She flinched at the hostility in his face

"Muir, you don't understand…" Cathy started.

"I understand one thing," he said, and her senses leaped in alarm as he dug his fingers into her shoulders and drew her toward him. "Your body talks to mine," he said, shaking her. "Every time we're together I'm aware of it. You can't hide it from me, whatever else you've hidden."

"Don't Muir," she whispered, trembling, and as his right hand slipped slowly down her arm to the strained tension of her breast, the shock of his touch made her breath catch in shuddered pleasure.

Muir's breathing quickened, his arms went around her and held her fiercely as his mouth found hers. Cathy kissed him back with something like desperation.

CHARLOTTE LAMB
is also the author of these

Harlequin Presents

and these

Harlequin Romances

Many of these books are available at your local bookseller.

For a free catalog listing all titles currently available,
send your name and address to:

HARLEQUIN READER SERVICE
1440 South Priest Drive, Tempe, AZ 85281
Canadian address: Stratford, Ontario N5A 6W2

CHARLOTTE LAMB

betrayal

Harlequin Books

TORONTO • NEW YORK • LOS ANGELES • LONDON
AMSTERDAM • PARIS • SYDNEY • HAMBURG
STOCKHOLM • ATHENS • TOKYO • MILAN

Harlequin Presents first edition April 1983
ISBN 0-373-10585-1

Original hardcover edition published in 1983
by Mills & Boon Limited

CHAPTER ONE

SHE had had to escape; the ballroom had been suffocatingly hot, and far too overcrowded, she hadn't been able to breathe, her head had ached and she had felt sure she was going to faint. That, at least, was what she told herself, mentally rehearsing the excuses she might have to give to Muir if he ran her to earth, but Cathy knew that there were other, more urgent reasons for her sudden overwhelming need to get away. It had all started so lightly, she hadn't meant to let it get out of hand. She still didn't know how it had happened, how she could have been so stupid, and she wished desperately that she could pretend to herself that it hadn't, but it was too late for that.

Or had it been too late from the minute she saw him? She closed her eyes, leaning on the balustrade of the terrace which ran behind the hotel, hating herself. Behind her she heard the crash of cymbals, the roll of drums and a roar of laughter. The dance would soon be over, it was gone eleven. Everyone was in a euphoric mood; it was the last night of the conference and tomorrow, after an early breakfast, Cathy would be flying home. She had managed to slip away from him in the ballroom while he was getting her a drink. All she had to do now was stay out of his way until she could get up to her room, then in the morning she would be gone before Muir got up.

'Oh, there you are!'

The voice made her whole body jerk in violent reaction. She stiffened, her hands closing over the cold stone of the balustrade, and had to take a long, deep breath before she could turn and smile. 'Oh, hello, Muir!'

'I've been hunting everywhere for you. What on earth are you doing out here?' He walked over towards her, a very tall man in evening clothes, the dark material giving an added force to his formidable face, in spite of the charm in his grey eyes and lazy smile. The first time they met, Cathy had been struck by the contradiction in his face. Muir had fascinated, puzzled, alarmed her on sight, and she had watched other women reacting in the same dazed way when they saw him.

'I was just coming back in,' she lied, moving hurriedly as though to go back into the ballroom.

Muir stepped in front of her, put both hands on the balustrade on either side of her, trapping her. 'Were we playing hide-and-seek?' he asked, his voice dropping to an intimate murmur which made the hair on the back of her neck prickle. 'Do I get a prize for finding you?'

Cathy felt him looking at her mouth, and a tremor of alarm ran through her. Dry-mouthed, she said: 'It was so hot in there—I just had to get some air, I couldn't breathe!'

'I thought you seemed breathless,' said Muir, mockery in his eyes, and her heart quickened. This was what she had fled from, it would be ironic if she had precipitated the very thing she dreaded. The lighthearted game which they had been playing all week had become something very different this evening. Suddenly she had had to admit how dangerously close they had come—dancing with him had become an intolerable intimacy, isolating them from everyone around them, she had been intensely aware of him and known that Muir was just as aware of her. On the surface they had talked and smiled, but the way he looked at her, moved against her as they danced, had keyed her up to an intolerable degree, and in the end she had fled.

This was worse, though; this was far more dangerous—out here they were alone under the dark night sky with only the stars to watch them.

'I only slipped out for a minute, there was so much noise. I'm tired, I suppose, it has been a hectic week.' It was the first conference Cathy had ever been to and she hoped it would be the last. If Hugh Brown had not been reckless enough to try to overtake a lorry on a difficult bend the night before he was due to fly out here, she would never have come at all. At such short notice Cathy had been the only member of staff Mrs Telford felt she could trust to come and represent the firm. Cathy knew most of what went on in the group because all the important decisions passed down from Mrs Telford, who kept her finger firmly on what happened in the hotel chain she had inherited from her dead husband. As Mrs Telford's private assistant, Cathy hadn't needed to be briefed on the various matters which her boss felt should be pressed during the conference sessions. It had been Cathy who had passed on Mrs Telford's views to Hugh Brown, the London manager of the group, and when he crashed his car Mrs Telford had catapulted Cathy into taking his place. It had seemed such fun at the start, Cathy had enjoyed it enormously, but now she wished she had never come.

'Shy, Cathy?'

She heard the smile in his voice and kept her head bent, not daring to look up because of what her eyes might tell him.

'Muir——' she began, then paused, unable to say what she knew she had to say. Her mind broke into little pieces every time she tried to explain to him, she was a coward, she just couldn't face it.

'I know,' he said, a deep rough note coming into his voice, but he didn't know, he had no idea, and it was not going to be easy to tell him. 'A bit like being hit by an avalanche, isn't it?'

Cathy forced a laugh. 'I wouldn't know, I've never been hit by one. Do you ski, Muir? I've never been to a skiing resort, is it fun? I've often wondered if . . .'

'Stop talking,' he said huskily, putting one hand under her chin and tipping her head back so that she felt the long, warm strands of her hair rustling against her red satin dress. Her hair was an unusual colour: too rich a shade to be blonde, too fair to be red, somewhere between the two, a warm amber gold. Muir's other hand reached up to touch it, his fingers gently tangling with the thick curls, and Cathy looked through her lowered lashes at him, her heart hurting in her chest.

'You look fantastic in that dress,' he said. 'I haven't been able to take my eyes off you all evening.'

'Thank you.' She had chosen the dress with

some care a few weeks back, for a dinner party.
The softly ruched collar flared out from the low
neckline with all the romantic glamour of a
Victorian evening dress and was matched by the
very tight, small waist and spreading, rustling
skirts which fell to her feet. Mrs Telford had raised
her eyebrows, pointing out that the vivid red of the
material was a risky colour for a blonde, but once
she had seen Cathy in it she had changed her
mind. Cathy had not bought the dress with Muir
in mind, of course, but she knew suddenly that she
would never be able to wear it without thinking of
him, remembering the way those dark grey eyes
looked down at her as she leaned against the
balustrade, her scarlet skirts shimmering against
the long, lean darkness of his own figure. 'You
look terrific yourself,' she said involuntarily, then
wished she hadn't said it.

That was how she had got into this snare, that
was how it had all begun, just a week ago today,
on the plane from London. She couldn't believe it
now, but she had not even noticed him for half an
hour. She had been sitting in the window seat,
staring out at the creamy swirl of clouds flowing
beneath the plane, when suddenly they had parted
and she had seen the gleam of blue water below
and sat up abruptly, giving an exclamation of
pleasure.

'Seen a U.F.O.?' an amused voice had asked,
and she had looked over her shoulder, laughing,
and seen Muir through a haze of gold, his hard
face sunlit.

'I don't believe in them,' Cathy had said, and a
twist of mockery had pulled at his mouth.

'What do you believe in?' he had asked drily, and she had shrugged.

'There isn't time to tell you—we'll be there in an hour.'

'My God,' he'd said, lifting fine black brows in a movement of sardonic disbelief, 'you take my breath away. It would take me two seconds to list the things I believe in.'

'Ah, a cynic,' Cathy had smiled, and he had watched her, his eyes narrowing on her smooth-skinned, oval face, cool speculation in the way he observed the amused green eyes, the finely modelled nose, the warm curve of her pink mouth.

'You've got a very sexy . . .' he had paused for a deliberate second or two, then added mockingly, 'voice.'

'Snap,' Cathy had said, and that was the moment when she should have drawn back and asked herself what the hell she thought she was doing, flirting with a total stranger like this, flirting with any man, come to that; but at that moment she had not been thinking about consequences or any future, she had been feeling free and lighthearted and very happy.

'Among other things,' Muir had added, then before she could react to that, had told her his name, 'I'm Muir Ingram—are you going to Nice on holiday?'

'No, business,' she had said. 'And my name is Cathy Winter. Why are you going to Nice?'

It had begun before she knew what was happening, one step at a time, each leading so casually, almost unnoticeably, to another; taking her daily deeper and deeper into trouble. At any stage she could have ended it with a few words, but she had told herself it didn't mean anything, it was just a pleasant holiday friendship. In a few days they would part, never to meet again, and it would hurt nobody in the meantime for her to talk to him in the laughing intimacy which she was trying to pretend was not flirtation.

It had been so long since Cathy had felt so carefree; she felt like someone who has suddenly grown wings, she found herself laughing all the time, the days had flown past far too fast and every second of every day had been charged with an electric excitement. She had forgotten what fun it could be to tease and be teased, to exchange secret smiles, have private jokes—she felt she was a different person. Not a stranger, this other personality had always been buried inside her, sealed behind a heavy weight of anxiety and care, but it had suddenly escaped and she had not had the strength of mind to force it back out of sight, so she had deceived herself, as much as she had deceived Muir. She had kept on telling herself that no harm would be done, it wouldn't really matter.

She had been a blind fool.

'What are you thinking about?' Muir asked, bringing her abruptly back to the starlit terrace, and the disturbing feel of his long fingers winding their way idly through her clustered hair. 'You've been somewhere else all evening. Is it because tonight's the last night?'

'I suppose so—endings are always sad,' she said.

'There isn't going to be an ending for us, Cathy,' Muir said very softly, with laughter in his voice. 'You didn't think I was going to walk away and

forget you, did you?' He came closer, his body in
full contact with hers a second later, his arm
sliding around her waist, and his smiling eyes
watched the curve of her mouth part on a soft
intake of breath as she tensed.

'Muir, there's something I've got to tell you,' she
began, and Muir whispered:

'There's a coincidence—I've got something to
tell you, too—I'm crazy about you.' He was
smiling, but the words were husky and Cathy's
eyes widened in shock.

She couldn't speak, she stood there helplessly
watching his mouth come closer, the warm male
line of it almost hypnotising her. She seemed to
have been waiting for eternity to feel it touch her
own. When it did she was dizzy with pleasure, her
arms went round his neck, her hands clenched in
the thick black hair, her mind clouding with a
desire which made her bones melt.

Once or twice he had lightly brushed his lips
against her hand, along her cheek, but they had
been casual caresses, given with laughter. This was
very different. It was what she had wanted while
they were dancing, she had known what was on
Muir's mind as his muscled thigh touched her, the
hard-angled cheek brushed her hair. They had
suddenly not been talking, after days of doing little
else, and the sexual tension between them had
been like an electric forcefield shutting out
everyone else in the room.

They kissed, eyes closed, bodies straining
towards each other as if to dissolve one into the
other, and Cathy shuddered with excitement and
passion. It hurt when Muir reluctantly detached

himself and looked down at her, breathing thickly, a dark red stain along the high angle of his cheekbones.

'Cathy, Cathy,' he whispered, 'if you knew what I was thinking!' His voice was unsteady, but it carried that smile which made her heart turn over. If she had felt nothing but this deep-burning sensual awareness it would not have been so dangerous—what frightened her was that desire for Muir came hand in hand with such real warmth.

Closing her eyes, she wished painfully that she had met him three years ago, or that she had never met him at all. He was going to hate her in a minute, and Cathy ached already, the pain so intense that she couldn't speak.

She felt his lips delicately laying a path to her ear, along her throat, teasing and intimate, then he said almost inaudibly: 'The dance is almost over, but we've got a whole night ahead of us. I couldn't sleep, could you? Why don't we go for a walk along the sea-front and talk? We've got to work out ways and means.'

'Ways and means?' She was too dazed to follow that and she heard him laugh.

'How are we going to see each other? You live down in the West Country, miles from London, and I'm always being despatched to the other end of the earth. One of us is going to have to change her job.'

'Muir. . . .'

He didn't let her finish the sentence, he completed it for her, as he imagined. 'I know, that was a sexist remark, I plead guilty, but surely the

Telford chain could switch you to their London office? There are no national newspapers down in Devon, I can't come to you. It will have to be the other way round.' His eyes smiled at her. 'You do want to see me whenever I can get a few hours free, don't you, Cathy?'

He waited for her to answer that, the certainty going out of his eyes as he watched her troubled face, and Cathy stood very still, gathering all her courage.

She had to force the words out; screwing them up from the depths of her body, so that they sounded hoarse.

'I'm engaged, Muir.' She couldn't even wrap it up, tell him lightly, she had left it far too late—she had to do it in three short words.

She watched his face change, his eyes widen, go almost black with shock while his skin lost colour and became grey, and swallowed, trembling, before the rest of it came pouring out of her—blurred, barely coherent, stammered in a shaky voice.

'I should have told you. I kept meaning to, but it never seemed the right moment. At first it didn't seem to matter, I didn't expect it to matter, there was no reason to mention it . . .'

'You don't wear a ring,' he broke in curtly, closing a hand over her left wrist and pulling up her hand to stare at her bare fingers.

'I haven't got it on,' Cathy stammered. 'It's a Victorian opal ring. I lost the centre stone last week and took it to a jeweller, he's trying to find a stone that matches the other two.'

'Why didn't you tell me?' Muir asked in a harsh

voice, frowning. 'What's his name?'

'Stephen Telford.'

'Telford?' The name broke out of him at white-hot speed, and she winced from the sudden tightening of his hand around her wrist.

'He's my boss's son,' she said, and Muir flung her hand away, turning to walk down the terrace in a fierce, aggressive stride which took him to one end and back again so quickly that she didn't have time to pull herself together before he was standing in front of her again. Starlight glittered on his face, showing her eyes as cold and sharp as the stars themselves.

'How long have you been engaged?'

'Two years,' she said, and saw Muir's face harden, his eyes narrowing.

'Two years?' he repeated incredulously. 'Why such a long engagement? Why haven't you married?' Then an icy, derisive smile twisted his mouth. 'Or can I guess? Mrs Telford doesn't want her son to marry her personal assistant, is that it? She doesn't think you're good enough for him.'

'No! It isn't like that at all.'

'Isn't it?' he asked with a contemptuous smile, before she could go on to explain. 'Then why the long engagement?' And before she could answer that, he broke out harshly: 'And why have you never mentioned him? A week, Cathy, a whole week! I've seen you every day, talked about everything under the sun, and you never breathed his name, not once. Don't tell me that was an accident, don't lie to me!' His voice had risen, deep and so angry it had a scalding heat in it. She felt sick under his bitter stare. 'You say you didn't think it mattered—what am I supposed to make of that? What you really mean is I didn't matter, you were just having a good time while you were on holiday, weren't you? You picked me up . . .'

'I didn't pick you up!' That stung for some reason, and she flushed, her lips quivering. 'If any picking up was done, you did it. You spoke first, on the plane—I hadn't even looked at you.'

His eyes hardened. 'You should have told me you were engaged to another man that first day . . .'

'Yes,' she admitted, 'I should have done.' She had known it then, she had known it ever since.

'But you didn't. You talked about Mrs Telford all the time and never mentioned her son.' His hand flashed out and grabbed her wrist again, he stared at her bare finger where the faint pallor betrayed that she had normally worn a ring there. 'Are you even engaged to him? Or is that a lie, too? Does he even exist?'

'Why should I invent an engagement or a man . . .' she began, and Muir snarled at her.

'Why should you . . .'

His words choked off as the ballroom door burst open and a laughing chain of people danced out, one behind the other, holding each other's waists while in the ballroom the band played a Conga. Faces peered towards them, one or two people waved, a thin man in a red cummerbund shouted: 'Come on, you two, stop kissing and join on the end!' The others laughed and someone else said: 'Nice work if you can get it, Muir—you must tell me your secret.'

'God!' Muir ground out in a low voice, pushing

her out of the way as the swaying line of dancers looped around them. A moment later Cathy felt herself being seized by a hand and propelled into the line with someone's hands on either side of her waist.

'Party pooper,' said the young man who had grabbed her. 'I'll report you to the union!'

Cathy let herself be carried away with them back into the ballroom, she felt Muir's angry eyes following, then the blaze of lights from the chandeliers dazzled her as she came out of the dark night, and she automatically fell into step as the chain wove in and out around the long room. When the dancing ended and everyone broke up, clapping and laughing, she was breathless, but she seized her chance to slide out of the open door into the hotel foyer. Almost running, she went up to the desk and got her key, and hurried back to the lift just as Muir shot through the ballroom door.

'Cathy!'

The lift doors had opened, she stepped inside and pressed the button, hearing his footsteps racing over the marble floor as the doors softly closed. Shaking, Cathy leaned against the steel wall, her arms folded across her trembling body, her eyes shut. When the lift stopped at her floor she was out of it and racing down the corridor at once. Muir had long legs and a very fit body, he would charge up the stairs three at a time—she had seen him do it only yesterday and laughed enviously.

She had just managed to get her door open, her hands shaking as she fumbled with her key, when she heard him coming. Running into the room, she slammed the door, bolted it and stood there, trembling, as she listened. It had hurt to see the contempt in his eyes, but it had only been what she expected—Muir couldn't despise her any more than she despised herself.

He rapped on the door with his knuckles, making her jump. 'Cathy! Open this door—if you think I'm letting it go at that, you're very wrong. I have a lot to say to you—open up!'

'Muir, don't,' she said huskily. 'Leave it, please let's just leave it . . .'

'I'm sure that's what you'd like, you cheating little bitch,' he snarled, 'but I'm not walking away without telling you what I think of you!'

'I know what you think of me,' she whispered, and his fist crashed against the door, making the wood vibrate. Cathy backed, biting her lip.

'Open this door—Cathy, do you hear me? Open this door!'

It was several minutes before she heard him walking away and she sagged in misery as she turned from the door. It hurt more than anything had ever hurt her before, but it was finished, and that was a strange sort of relief. Cathy had hated knowing that she was living a lie every time she was with him. At least she had told him the truth at last.

Walking over to the windows, she threw open the shutters and leaned on the sill, staring up at the stars. How beautiful, she thought; warm and cloudless, the sky moved above her with such serenity, the air scented with flowers and filled with the whirr of cicadas and the slow waltz music from the ballroom, and it was a bitter contrast to the aching fever in her veins, the restless, tormented yearning she felt and had felt all evening.

She lifted her thick cluster of hair in both hands, letting the air flow over her nape. It was so warm, how would she ever sleep?

The phone rang and she froze. For a moment while it shrilled, she stared at it uncertainly. It was probably Muir, but it could be Mrs Telford—she had rung every evening so far, but she had not rung tonight. Cathy had assumed that that was because she would be flying home tomorrow. She let it ring a few more times, then slowly went over to pick it up.

'We have to talk, you know that,' said Muir without prefacing the harshly delivered words, and her hand trembled as she held the phone.

'Muir, there's no point.'

'Cathy——' he began, then stopped. She heard him breathing and a tear crept under her eyelid; she angrily brushed it away.

'Please, don't hate me, I didn't expect it would get so serious. I didn't mean it to, I . . .'

Muir interrupted her in a voice which was only just controlled. 'Tell me one thing, that's all I want to know now—do you love him?'

That Cathy could answer with total honesty and the quick note of her voice held relief. 'Yes, yes, I do, Muir, I do love him—you see . . .' There was so much more she could say, but Muir did not wait to hear it. His voice was almost inaudible, yet carried the bitter weight of a contempt which slashed into her like a knife.

'Then thank God you don't pretend to love me!'

The phone went down with such force that her ear sang with the noise for minutes afterwards. She slowly replaced her own receiver and sat down on the bed. She put her hands over her eyes, pressing her palms firmly into them to ease the hot ache behind the eyeballs, and saw Muir in the plane that first day, with the sun on his brown skin, smiling. She should have been warned then, looking at that formidable and very masculine face. She should have realised what utter folly it was to let herself pretend even for one moment to be free, she should have told him all about Stephen, if she had done so at the start everything would have been different. They could have been friends, talked lightly, had fun dancing each evening, without any of the slowly building emotion which had flared up so disastrously tonight. If she had set out the rules, put up the boundaries, made it clear that he had to keep outside them, he wouldn't now be hating her.

She searched in her handbag for some aspirins, took two with some water, then undressed and took a shower before finishing the packing she had started that afternoon between the last session and the time she had spent getting ready for the Gala evening.

It took her some time to get to sleep. She was up when her breakfast tray arrived and as soon as she had drunk some orange juice and a cup of black coffee went down to pay her bill. Her taxi arrived five minutes later and she drove away to Nice airport in a state of weary depression, but grateful for the fact that she had managed to leave the hotel without running into Muir again. Her most pressing worry had been that he might be up and they might meet—that would have been too unbearable.

It was lunchtime when she got back to Westoak and she took a taxi from the railway station, straight to the office, knowing that Mrs Telford would expect an immediate de-briefing session. The streets were crowded, it took the taxi driver some time to make his way through the thick traffic and he grumbled in a casual way over his shoulder.

'Time they did something about this traffic—chronic, that's what it is, they keep talking about a one-way system, but nothing gets done.'

Cathy leaned back, staring towards the distant hills which ringed the town, their profile veiled in smoky blue mist today, a heat haze which was lifting very gradually. Westoak lay in a flat, fertile green valley threaded by a low-lying river and on summer days the surrounding hills seemed to capture the sunlight and imprison it between them so that the valley was humid and suffocatingly warm.

'Where you been, then?' the driver asked, and with a start, she told him.

'Nice?' he repeated, grinning round at her. 'Nice for some.'

Cathy managed to smile, and, encouraged, he asked: 'Holiday, was it? Doesn't seem to have done you much good, if you don't mind me saying so—you look a bit peaky, darling.'

'Do I?' Cathy's head was hammering and she wondered how much longer it was going to take to get to the office.

'Had a bit too much sun?' he asked. 'Or did you get some tummy trouble? I always get it abroad, it's the water, you know, never drink the water, full of bugs it is.'

'Yes,' said Cathy on a note of relief as the taxi pulled into the drive leading up to the office. The driver handed her case over, accepted the money she gave him and drove off. She carried her case through the glass doors into the cool foyer and across to the lift. While she was waiting for it to come down from the top floor, someone came hurrying up behind her.

'Hi, you're back, have a good time? You lucky pig, imagine a whole week at Nice at the firm's expense—why doesn't it happen to me?'

'Hallo, Jennie,' Cathy said, and the other girl looked at her curiously, her enormous dark brown eyes opened very wide. Jennie was myopic but would not wear her glasses except when she was actually working, so that she tended to peer at you uncertainly until she was up close enough to be sure it was you. She was not unlikely to walk straight into desks, either, or to be seen earnestly apologising to a coat rack. Cathy had saved her from imminent death on a number of occasions, dragging her back from under the wheels of cars by her sleeve. Small, slight, dark, she was inclined to a sarcasm which could be goodhumoured enough when directed at a friend, but could be sharp enough to cut when she used it on someone she did not like.

As they walked into the lift, Jennie asked: 'Was it a successful conference? Strike that question—I

never heard of a conference which was successful.
Did you enjoy it, anyway?'

'It was great,' said Cathy with lacklustre
enthusiasm, pushing a wandering strand of hair
back from her cheek.

'You look terrible,' Jennie observed, her eyes
screwed up as she leaned closer to check Cathy's
expression. 'Tired? You surely haven't got jet-lag
just flying from the South of France, or was it the
train journey that was killing? I know how you
feel, I often think it would be faster by
wheelbarrow.' She paused, then said: 'Hey, are
you with me? Or am I talking to myself?'

Cathy pulled herself together. 'Sorry, my mind's
a mess today.'

'Well, you said it,' Jennie murmured drily. 'Far be
it from me to contradict you, but what's unusual
about that? What's on your mind, anyway?'

Cathy shrugged. 'Oh, Stephen, I suppose,' she
said with enough truth to make it sound frank.

'If this is what getting married does to you I'm
glad I'm staying single,' Jennie teased. 'Not that I
have the chance of doing otherwise unless I can get
Mike in an armlock one dark night and force a
submission!'

'You don't want to marry Mike,' Cathy said
without stopping to think, and got a dry look.

'Don't I? Thanks for telling me. I might not
have worked that out for myself.'

'Okay, touchy!' Cathy retorted, half in apology,
half teasingly. She and Jennie had been to school
together, there was very little they did not know
about each other, and Cathy was well aware how
prickly Jennie could be about her private life.

Secretive, feline, she often reminded Cathy of a cat with barely sheathed claws ready to spit at anyone who came too close. 'I just gathered that you weren't taking him too seriously, that's all—the last time you mentioned him you called him a big dummy.'

A rueful smile flashed over Jennie's face. 'Did I? What a memory! I'll have to watch you. Mike's okay, I like him more than anyone else I've been dating lately, but you're right, clever, he doesn't make me feel I'm flying.' She laughed. 'Remember you once said that being in love makes you feel you're flying without an aeroplane?'

Cathy was relieved for once that Jennie could only see what was right in front of her nose. If she had been wearing her glasses and able to see Cathy's face she might have picked up something of what Cathy was feeling. As it was, Cathy managed to control her voice, answer lightly, managing to laugh. 'And you said you always got travel-sick when you flew, so maybe you should never fall in love!'

'Always practical,' Jennie agreed as the lift stopped and the doors opened. 'See you,' she said, stepping out and automatically turning left towards the Publicity Office where she worked. As the lift doors closed, Cathy heard a crash and Jennie saying in an agitated voice: 'Sorry,' then the rattle of a trolley and the clink of cups. 'Why don't you watch where . . .' a voice began just before the lift whisked Cathy upwards, smiling to herself.

She was still smiling as she walked into Mrs Telford's office and the woman behind the desk looked up and smiled back. 'Cathy! How did it go?

Flight okay? Have a good trip back?'

The quick, succinct rattle of questions was typical of the woman and Cathy smiled wryly at her. 'Everything was fine.' She glanced at the girl sitting on a chair in front of the desk, a shorthand pad open on her knee. 'Am I interrupting? Hi, Carol.'

Mrs Telford's secretary breathed in a husky voice: 'Hi, nice to have you back, Cathy.' She had only worked for Mrs Telford for a month and was doing a very good impression of being super-efficient, jumping to answer phones or get files which Mrs Telford suddenly demanded, typing perfectly at speed, not only staying late but arriving early, and always with an expression of alert concentration on her face. Her brown hair was slightly fluffy, very fine and inclined to be all over the place when she had washed it, but she spent a lot of time sternly combing it back into a neat style curling around her face, and her hazel eyes were wide apart and very wide awake. Sometimes when she was working, Cathy would suddenly feel herself being watched and look up to find Carol eyeing her with the eager anticipation of a bird waiting for a worm to pop up out of the ground. On her first day at the firm, Carol had asked her ingenuously if she would stop work when she got married, leaving Cathy in no doubt that, if and when she did, Carol would apply for her job. There was something slightly unnerving about standing in shoes someone else wanted to fill. If Cathy had been the ambitious type herself she might have been irritated by Carol's eager beaver smile, but as it was Carol amused her.

'We'll leave the dictation for now, Carol,' Mrs Telford said, closing the folder in front of her. Handing it to her secretary, she added: 'I'll buzz when I want you.'

Carol said in that breathless little voice: 'Yes, Mrs Telford, certainly. I'll get on with typing the letters you've dictated, shall I?'

'You do that,' said Mrs Telford as the girl walked to the door.

Cathy sank down into the vacated chair, linking her hands behind her head. Mrs Telford stared at her. 'You look tired—conference too much for you? You sounded all right on the phone while you were there.' There was the faintest touch of impatience in the voice now—Mrs Telford had no time for people who fell down on the job or were delicate in health. She was capable of great kindness and extreme generosity, but being apparently made of plated steel herself she could never understand why anyone else should be less durable. Even when she had had to have a serious operation, she had amazed the medical staff by forcing herself out of bed within twenty-four hours—it had only been for a moment, she had had to get straight back into it, but the Ward Sister had told Cathy that her boss must be some sort of Superwoman, then added thoughtfully: 'Or a maniac—she was in no state to move an inch.' The ferocious energy which had driven her to become a formidable businesswoman had, oddly, only showed itself since her husband's death. Cathy's childhood memories of her were quite different—tiny, with fine delicate bone structure and sleek dark hair, she had been very much a background figure in John Telford's life, an elegant home-maker and hostess to his friends and business acquaintances, a gentle, soft-spoken mother to Stephen and his brother David, a very female woman on the surface. Cathy had often wondered if it had been her husband's death or that of her younger son which had altered her. David had died of polio which he had contracted during a foreign holiday, and in the eight years since his death, Cathy had almost never heard his mother mention him. If his name came up in family conversation, Mrs Telford fell silent—and such a silence could only mean a pain so deep she could not bear to have it touched.

'I went to bed very late and had to get up at first light to get that plane,' Cathy told her now. 'I'm dead on my feet, but I thought you'd want to have a chat about what was said in that last session.'

'Give me a quick rundown now, then you can incorporate the details into the report you'll be doing—I'd like that by next Wednesday. There's a board meeting on Friday, I'd like to have copies of your reports run off and circulated to all the members for discussion at the meeting.' Mrs Telford smiled across the desk, her face softening. 'Stephen's missed you, so have I. It's nice to have you back.'

Cathy smiled at her. 'It's nice to be back.'

Mrs Telford was not a woman who allowed sentiment to cloud her mind for long. 'Good,' she said. 'Now, how did that last session go?'

When she left the office, Cathy stopped off to have a quick, light lunch before she took a taxi to the Telford house. Her car was parked in the garage at her own home, but she wanted to see Stephen as soon as possible.

The front door was opened by a short, dumpy little figure in a dark green dress. Cathy smiled at her. 'Hallo, Nandy,' she said, knowing that the cross face would not smooth out and knowing, too, that Nandy's scowling exterior was no guide to her heart. Time and experience had marked those square-cut features in a criss-crossed map of lines, nature had given her the sullen outward pout of the mouth, the solid beaky nose, the currant-like eyes. Under all that, Nandy hid a gentleness and tenderness she would go to the stake to deny in public, while in private it was expressed in everything she did, particularly with Stephen, whom she adored. It was mutual. Stephen loved his aunt, he always had, but now he loved her even more after two years of a childlike dependency on her which only Nandy's casual manner had made bearable for him.

'We were wondering where you were,' Nandy said. 'Thought you'd be back hours ago.'

'I had to go to the office first.'

'Well, you'd better tell Stephen that yourself,' Nandy said almost threateningly. 'He's in his room.'

Cathy knew that the gruff voice and scowl hid a delicate tact—Nandy was giving them some time alone. 'Right, I'll go up,' she said, and ran up the stairs.

Stephen was sitting by the open window, the room full of the heady fragrance of the roses massed below, the dusty brown of his hair winnowed by a faint breeze as he turned his head towards the door. 'Cathy, you're back!' His hazel eyes had his mother's shape and size but looked much larger in his thin, pale face. Cathy stood there, smiling at him, while he ran a satisfied gaze over her.

'You've got a tan. It suits you, we must send you to conference more often!'

She moved to join him, and he said quickly: 'No, stand there!' His thin hands took a grip on the arms of the chair and Cathy watched tensely as he heaved himself out of it, his legs visibly trembling. He straightened, let go of the chair and took a step towards her, then another, his features tight with concentration. He looked to her like a baby learning to walk, a shaky toddler, fixing its eyes on its mother, and her heart moved painfully inside her.

'That's wonderful, darling!' she said, taking the last step to meet him.

'You're not crying? Cathy, you idiot!' He put his arms round her and she hid her face on his shoulder, deeply aware of the fine-boned fragility of his body under the thin shirt. Two years ago, Stephen had been lean and very fit, a busy, active young man with a lively personality. Now he was quiet, contemplative, his whole mind given to the struggle back to health. They had both changed beyond recognition during those two years.

'Stephen,' she said with fierce urgency, 'don't let's wait any longer! You're going to walk soon, I know you are—let's get married right away!'

For a moment he didn't answer, his cheek against her hair. 'Please, Stephen,' she begged. 'Why don't we fix a date? You're so much better, it seems silly to put our wedding off for another year.'

Stephen had his mother's strong-minded determination to do things his own way, as well as a streak of obstinate pride which made him hard to shift once he had made up his mind. When he crashed his car a few weeks after he and Cathy had got engaged he had first tried to insist on breaking their engagement. At that stage the doctors had been saying Stephen would be paralysed for life—in the crash he had broken almost every bone in his body and Cathy knew it had been a miracle of sheer determination, both on his part and on that of the medical staff in the intensive care unit in which he had been nursed, which had pulled him through. Cathy had refused pointblank to give him back his ring. She had gone on refusing after he was brought home on a stretcher to spend what Stephen himself believed would be the rest of his life in a bed or a wheelchair. Nandy had given up her job in a London hospital to come and live in Westoak and nurse him. Stephen had only accepted her help because he and Nandy had always had a close bond, during his childhood he had been closer to her than to his mother, who had not always managed to hide her preference for her younger son, David. Stephen's illness had changed his relationship with his mother, brought them much closer. Mrs Telford had been terrified of losing him after having lost both the husband she had adored and her other son. The family had moved together in a tight-knit weave of which Cathy had become an essential part in the two years since Stephen's crash—she would have married him at any time during those two years, but Stephen had been insistent that he would only marry her when he could walk down the aisle.

Now she felt a thrust of anxiety, a prickle of something approaching fear. 'Please, let's get married now, Stephen,' she said again when he stayed silent.

'No,' Stephen said on a deep sigh. 'No, darling—we'll get married when I can walk. That's what I've been working towards for the past two years, we won't change our goal now.'

Cathy bit her lip, closing her eyes. She felt Stephen kissing her ear. A smile sounded in his voice. 'Right? You understand, don't you, Cathy?' he asked, and without looking up she nodded, but there was nervous tension in the uneasy tremor of her mouth as she leaned her face against him, making sure she kept her expression out of his view.

CHAPTER TWO

'CAN you give me a lift home tonight?'

Cathy glanced up from the file she was studying, and smiled at Jennie. 'Of course, but I thought you had a date with Mike? Change of plans?'

Jennie wandered into the office and perched on the side of Cathy's desk, her skirt hitched up to display her slim legs. 'He just rang to say he couldn't make it.'

Something in her tone alerted Cathy, who watched her face. 'Having trouble with him?' Jennie's love life was always up and down, like a see-saw.

'It isn't the first time he's cancelled a date at the last minute,' Jennie said with a defiant little smile. She very rarely confided in Cathy and when she did Cathy always had to work hard to get out of her what Jennie both wanted to talk about and was reluctant to admit. The combination of a secretive pride and a dislike of admitting emotion made Jennie someone who was not easy to get to know, and only the years they had known each other made it possible for Cathy to catch the occasional glimpse of what was going on under the surface of Jennie's tart and assured exterior.

'Is he very busy at work?'

'I doubt it,' Jennie said drily. Mike was a local photographer who seemed to work in fits and

32

starts. 'I suspect his private life is very busy,' she added, picking up the framed photograph of Stephen standing on Cathy's desk and regarding it as if she had never seen it before.

'Someone else?' Cathy asked tentatively, frowning as she closed the file in front of her and tapped one long pearl-tipped finger on top of it.

'That's my guess,' shrugged Jennie, replacing the picture of Stephen. 'There wasn't much fire in the first place, but whatever there was has definitely cooled lately.' She gave Cathy a grimace. 'Lucky I wasn't crazy over him, isn't it?'

'Maybe if you had been . . .' Cathy begun, then cut off the sentence, wishing she had never started it, as Jennie gave her a long, cool stare.

'He wouldn't be legging it for the wide, open spaces and someone else, you mean? Well, maybe, who knows?' She leaned over the desk to study the label on the front of the file. 'That the conference report? I read it yesterday—stirring stuff, you made it sound like a lot of fun. I reckon the only reason they have them is so that they can live it up at the firm's expense for a few days. Nothing much ever seems to come out of them except a few ruined livers and the odd guilty secret.' She looked at Cathy and smiled, and for some stupid reason Cathy felt herself flushing, although it was absurd to wonder if Jennie had guessed that something had happened while Cathy was in Nice. Jennie looked at her oddly as she slid down to the floor and turned towards the door. 'Oh, well, back to the grindstone,' she said as she walked away.

'I'll pick you up at six,' Cathy called to her back.

'Fine, see you.' Jennie went out, closing the door behind her, and Cathy's eyes went to the studio photograph of Stephen. It had been taken before the accident—he was more than two years younger, his brown hair glossy and smooth above his smiling face, the hazel eyes, so much like his mother's, full of life and vigour. Since the photo had been taken he had lost a great deal of weight, he was several stones lighter, his body seeming fleshless. He had a'ways been a very lively, active man, playing tennis in summer and swimming frequently, visiting the gym several times a week. It made her heart ache to think of him as he was now.

Westoak was a small country town; everyone who lived there knew everybody else by sight, if not by name, and Cathy had the advantage of coming from a family who had lived in the district for generations. Her father was headmaster of the local secondary school, her uncle had been the senior surgeon at the town's only hospital until his early death from heart failure a year ago. The family were very far from being wealthy. Cathy and her father lived in a small cottage on the outskirts of the town, just half a mile from Garth House, where the Telfords lived. She had known Stephen most of her life, they had played together as children and grown up together. Stephen had gone to boarding school, of course, but during the summer holidays he had often had tuition from George Winter in Latin and mathematics. Stephen was not academic, he found his school work difficult and boring, and he had not been very fond of Cathy's father.

George Winter was a highly respected man in the town, but he was a very tough headmaster, and there was a certain amount of alarm mingled with the respect in which he was held, particularly by those who had been his pupils. He did not mince his words, nor was it easy to pull the wool over his eyes. People tended to be wary of arguing with him; when he was angry he could become chilling. Cathy loved her father, but she was half afraid of him, too, always aware that she had never reached the high standards he had set for her. Neither had Stephen—it had been a bond between them. Stephen had respected George Winter, too, but he had been relieved to dive out of the headmaster's study into his large, wild garden to find Cathy and play rounders or badminton with her.

Stephen was five years older, he had shot ahead into adulthood while Cathy was still in plaits and gymslips and for some years they had not met, but soon after she began working at the headquarters of the Telford group, which was based in Westoak, where they had had their first large hotel and where the family lived, she had met Stephen again and he had asked her to be his partner at the firm's annual dance. They had been dating for a year before Stephen got around to asking her to marry him, and Cathy had been worried about his mother's reaction. After all, Cathy had neither money nor position, she was a very ordinary girl, while Stephen would one day be the major stockholder in a company which was expanding at a mushroom rate.

Mrs Telford had been surprisingly nice about it,

perhaps because she had had a year during which to get used to the idea that her son was going to marry a member of her own staff. Cathy had been given a guarded welcome, although she could not exactly say that Stephen's mother had rolled out the red carpet for her. Their engagement had been announced shortly after Cathy's twenty-first birthday. Stephen had, by then, been twenty-six. Since the accident he had looked much older; his face drawn and white from hours of pain, his eyes shadowed and bruised, his brown hair dry and lifeless from the months of lying in a bed.

Cathy could not put her finger on the moment when her feelings about Stephen had altered—it had happened so gradually, over the long months, and it had been disguised even from her by deep affection for him, a fondness which remained intact despite the change in her, in both of them. She still loved Stephen, she knew she always would, but for a long time her pulses had not missed a beat when she saw him, she had not felt the tremulous, dangerous excitement she had felt in Muir Ingram's arms.

She had not even understood the difference until she danced with Muir that evening. There was a whole world between loving someone with the warm tenderness she felt for Stephen, and knowing that just to be with someone was to be fully, painfully alive, as she was with Muir. The sensual ache she had felt while she danced with Muir, the intense awareness of his glance, his voice, the touch of his hand, had never been part of how she felt about Stephen. She had mistaken her own emotions when she believed herself to be in love

with Stephen—but she had only known that when
she discovered that Muir's effect on her was so
disturbing.

She put her hands over her face, a smothered
groan breaking from her. She despised herself for
what had happened. She had betrayed Stephen,
she had betrayed Muir—and it made her feel sick
if she contemplated the thought of Stephen ever
finding out how close she had come to starting an
affair with another man.

Stephen needed her, as much now as ever. If he
was ever to walk again, his psychotherapist had
once told her, he must be strongly motivated—
and Cathy had been his main motive from the
start. She had kept nagging him to work at his
exercises, to strengthen his leg muscles and spine,
the necessary preliminary if he was ever to walk,
and she was perfectly aware that Stephen had
driven himself onward when he was exhausted,
depressed, in a state of hopeless despair, because
he had been so determined to walk down the
aisle on their wedding day. She did not need to
think twice about what would happen if she
deserted him, if he ever felt she did not care
whether he walked or not, because on one very
bad night, a year ago, Stephen had told her,
clutching her hand so tightly that her fingers
were cramped and sore for a long time afterwards.
His voice husky and shaking, he had said: 'If
it wasn't for you I'd give up now, give up. I've
got those sleeping tablets in the drawer, I look at
them sometimes and think; well, that's one way
out . . .'

'Don't, Stephen!' she had cried out in fear and

pain, and he had kissed her hand, leaving the moist smear of tears along her palm.

'I've got more guts, darling. I think about you and then I grit my teeth and go on hoping—you're what I live for, Cathy, I keep going just by imagining the day I walk down the aisle towards you.'

She had clung to his hand, biting her lip, and been glad at the time, but now she felt the heavy load of guilt weighing her down every time she saw Stephen. It was three weeks since the conference, but she had not been able to get Muir out of her mind, he haunted her, not least because he had brought home to her so sharply her own state of frustration.

Living day by day with Stephen's illness, absorbed in his fight to walk again, burying herself in her job when she was not with him, she had not realised until she met Muir just how much she longed to be in a man's arms, how much she missed the laughing intimacies of a light flirtation, the piercing tension of a touch, a kiss.

She had left for that conference so hurriedly, off balance in the surprise of it. It was the first holiday she had had since Stephen's accident. She had spent all her free time with him over the past two years, and for so long Stephen had not smiled, let alone laughed, he had been far too ill.

On the plane to France she had felt oddly free, released from the long months of lonely anxiety, and she had not been able to resist Muir's smile and teasing small talk. She had been fascinated by his talk of his job—he was attending the conference, too, but as a journalist who had been sent to report on it for his daily paper, the *Globe*. He had amused her with talk of other conferences he had attended, all of them boring, she gathered. He had winked at her during dull sessions as she tried to stay awake and had passed her lively little cartoons of various members of the platform executive, showing them as animals: a sleepy pig in a floral dress, a long hissing snake in a collar and tie, a dormouse in a blue dress—herself, she had realised with a stifled giggle. Muir had made the conference come alive for her. She had known it was a dangerous game she was playing, but all the time she had told herself it didn't mean anything, it would soon be over and Muir, like herself, was only flirting lightly without any intention of getting seriously involved.

She had known her mistake that night at the dance. It would not have mattered so much that she had been feverishly aware of him if she had not been forced to recognise that Muir felt the same way. It was more than just a brief holiday romance—for both of them. Muir's eyes had told her so.

The phone rang, startling her out of her misery, and she stiffened before she controlled herself enough to pick it up. 'Hallo?'

'Cathy? Have you got the files on that new hotel in York? I thought I had them, but Carol tells me they aren't in the office.' Mrs Telford sounded irritable.

'Yes, I have them on my desk now, shall I bring them along?'

'I wish you wouldn't take files out of the cabinet without telling Carol you're doing it,' Mrs Telford snapped.

'I did tell her,' said Cathy. 'She must have forgotten.' I bet she did, she thought—it wasn't the first time Carol had 'forgotten' a message Cathy had given her.

'Well, bring them here *now*.' The phone went down and Cathy slowly replaced her own, frowning. She could do without that sort of hassle from Carol, she thought, as she gathered up the files on the latest Telford project and got up.

When she walked into the outer office leading to Mrs Telford's room, Carol gave her a wide-eyed apologetic smile. 'I'm terribly sorry, I just don't remember you taking them, it's my fault, I'm sure, but are you certain you mentioned it to me? Maybe you meant to and forgot.'

Cathy gave her a dry look. 'I have a very good memory,' she said, walking towards Mrs Telford's door.

Carol sprang into her path and seized the files, her voice dripping polite poison. 'I'll take them, she's in conference.'

Cathy had a good mind to insist on delivering them in person, but thought better of it, she just couldn't be bothered to get bogged down in a silly argument.

'Okay,' she said, releasing her grip on the files, and swung on her heel.

Satisfied with this tiny victory, Carol said: 'Have you heard about the big scare that's on in the town? People were talking about nothing else in the canteen at lunch, I'll be sure to walk home with someone, won't you?'

'What are you talking about?' Cathy asked, pausing with a frown to look back at her.

'Haven't you heard about it?' Carol leaned on her desk, her face flushed, looking excited.

'I didn't eat in the canteen, the food's terrible,' said Cathy, and Carol looked over her shoulder at Mrs Telford's door.

'Oh, I think it's pretty good,' she said, so loudly that Mrs Telford would have had to be deaf to avoid hearing. 'I always eat in the canteen, it's such good value for money.'

Cathy eyed her derisively and she looked away, then went on hurriedly; 'You know that redhead in the typists pool? Daphne?'

'Yes,' Cathy said patiently.

'Her sister's a nurse at St Andrew's—she lives in the nurses' home, the one down by the river near the bridge . . .'

'I know where you mean,' Cathy said, poised to leave and wondering when they were going to get to the point of the story. Whatever it was, it seemed to be exciting Carol a good deal, her eyes were fever-bright and she was speaking breathlessly.

'Well, last night a man broke in there—one of the nurses heard someone outside her door and looked out and he jumped her . . .'

'My God,' Cathy exclaimed, startled. 'How terrible!'

'She was petrified, Daphne says—it was a friend of her sister, one of the staff nurses, a pretty girl, Daphne said. She managed to scream and a couple of girls came out of their rooms and the man ran off—apparently he climbed down from the roof, they found a rope ladder dangling.'

'Have the police any idea who it was?'

'If they have, they haven't said anything. The nurses have all been warned to be on their guard. The police think he'll try again.'

'He took an awful risk, breaking into a place like a nurses' home,' Cathy commented, frowning. 'He must have known there were going to be a lot of people about.'

'He's mad, obviously,' Carol shuddered. 'Isn't it ghastly? None of us will be able to feel safe until they catch him. I've asked Peter to walk home with me tonight. I live down near the river and some of those streets are very quiet. I'd be too scared to walk home on my own.'

'Oh, I think you'd be safe enough in broad daylight,' Cathy said absently, and Carol shook her head vehemently.

'I'm not taking any chances. You want to be careful, too, Cathy.'

'I will,' said Cathy, walking to the door. As she made her way down the corridor she ran into the chief security officer of the building who stopped to ask if she had heard about the attempted rape at the nurses home.

'If you work late over the next few days make sure you let me know,' he said. 'We're going to have to be extra careful with security until this guy's caught.'

'He isn't likely to break into a block of offices,' Cathy said drily, and Mr Hughes looked at her with something like disapproval in his lined face.

'You can't be too careful.'

'I suppose not,' Cathy agreed, smiled at him and went on her way. No doubt it satisfied some craving in the human psyche to fly into a panic over one small incident, but she couldn't help wondering why they were all so fascinated by disaster. Perhaps their lives were so dull and quiet that they grabbed at the chance to feel a new emotion, even if it was only fear. Maybe the man who had broken into the nurses' home had been a burglar, or had been looking for a girl-friend he had quarrelled with—but whatever his reason he had given Westoak something to talk about for once.

That evening as she drove Jennie home, the break-in at the nurses' home was their chief topic of conversation. Jennie said that it was all over the town—she had heard about it from the lift attendant and people in her office as well as from a woman in a shop she had popped into at lunchtime.

'Maybe that's what Mike's up to these days,' she said, and Cathy laughed and gave her a wry look.

'I shouldn't say that to anyone but me— I know you're joking, but people have such vivid imaginations; they might take you seri-ously.'

'Poor Mike,' said Jennie, with a wicked glance at her, then said: 'No, you're right, I'll watch my tongue. When one of these whirlwind scares is on, people do get the craziest notions!'

Cathy drew up outside Jennie's home, a grey brick terraced house within walking distance of where Cathy and her father lived. 'See you tomorrow,' she said as Jennie got out of the car and her friend lifted a hand in a cheerful wave.

Cathy drove on to her own home and parked

the car outside the gate on the narrow grass verge. She walked up the paved path, hearing music from the sitting-room windows. Her father always arrived back from school between five and six and always unwound to music—he had a large library of classical records and played his way through them until he started again with his oldest and favourite piece of music—a well-worn recording of Heifetz playing a Bach violin concerto. George Winter was a man of settled habits. The death of his wife had sealed him into a cold shell of custom and formality—Cathy had never managed to get close to him. She had tried, but they just weren't on the same wavelength.

'Is that you, Cathy?' her father called as she paused outside the sitting-room door, and she went in, her face surprised.

'Yes, of course.' Who had he been expecting? she wondered, until he said. 'I must be jumpy after all this stupid talk.'

'Oh, you've heard about the break-in, have you?' Cathy asked as the music came to a stop and the record player switched itself off.

'My staff were talking of nothing else all day. I hope the police catch this fellow quickly—I remember what it was like last year when we had someone lurking around the schools in the town. Sheer panic—half the children took the chance to stay off school and we had the devil's own job persuading their parents that it was quite safe so long as the children didn't talk to strangers.' George Winter got up, his grey hair glinting in the light from the window, and changed the record. He was a distinguished-looking man, erect and well preserved, but the coldness of his usual expression detracted from his good looks. He would be retiring in five years, but he was not looking forward to it, Cathy sensed. His whole world revolved around the school, the town, his daily routine.

'What's for supper?' he asked, and she moved back to the door.

'Salad and cold chicken—there should be enough left from yesterday. It won't be long.'

She always did the cooking and the housework, although her father was always back hours before her—George Winter saw domestic tasks as falling within a woman's province and had never so much as offered to dry up after a meal. Cathy had never dreamt of asking him to, either. Sometimes, when she was very tired, she felt a flicker of rebellion about it, but she did not have the energy or the courage to argue it out with her father. While she was away, her father had got one of the neighbours to come in and do the housework. He had either eaten out or made himself cold meals.

Half an hour later she drove over to see Stephen, as she did each day. After months of seeming to get nowhere he was improving by leaps and bounds. He had been able to walk in a slow shuffle with the help of his stick long ago, but now he was beginning to walk without it. At present it was only a few steps, then he would have to sit down again, but it was amazing progress compared to the setbacks and disappointments of the previous year.

Cathy sat talking to him in his bedroom, his stereo playing softly and the window open to allow the warm night air to breathe around the room. Just before she left, Stephen shuffled over to the window with her and they leaned there, looking up at the moon. 'I feel stronger every day,' Stephen said, his face relaxed.

'You look it—we'll have you playing tennis next summer.'

He laughed. 'That will give you the chance you've been waiting for—you'll be able to beat me hollow.'

'How did you guess?' she teased. 'Revenge is sweet—how many times have you had me running all over the court like a lunatic? I insist you play with me first off before you get back on form, at least I'll be able to boast I did beat you once!'

He turned his head and kissed her, and Cathy stroked his hair as he drew away. 'You always make me feel so sure I can do it,' Stephen said on a sigh.

'Of course you can, I'm going to make sure you do.' She slipped her arm around his waist and walked back with him to his bed, watched as he wearily got into it and lay down. Cathy had helped him off with his robe, which she now held over her arm.

'Shall I close the window and draw the curtains?' she asked, and Stephen nodded. Cathy went back to the window, shut it, pulled the curtains together. 'Goodnight, darling,' she said, kissed him and went out, hearing the click of his bedside lamp as she shut the door.

Mrs Telford came out of the sitting-room just as Cathy reached the foot of the stairs, and said: 'Come and have a cup of coffee—I want to talk to you.'

Cathy followed her across the high-ceilinged hall, her footsteps clicking on the tiled floor. Garth House had been built a hundred years ago; apparently by someone who admired the architecture of railway stations. The Gothic battlements and twin turrets of the house were matched by huge, echoing rooms which were beseiged by draughts, winter and summer alike, the garden was full of gloomy laurel bushes which shut out the light from the lower floor and, after rain, dripped for hours in melancholy persistence. The house lay in a rectangle of lawns and trees, the stone walls surrounding it slightly crumbling now, their crevices sprouting ferns and wallflowers, ivy twining around the ancient hornbeams along the wall, strangling them in a possessive embrace. Even on a hot summer day the atmosphere was oppressive. You felt shut in, claustrophobic, imprisoned by dark green leaves and stone, and although the garden was full of birds they were often invisible, their presence only betrayed by rustlings among the undergrowth. Thick clouds of black flies danced on the air below the branches of the trees, you could not walk anywhere without beating them off. In the autumn when the leaves dropped and the skeletal trees creaked in the wind, great colonies of spiders spun dusty webs from branch to branch. Cathy liked neither the house nor the garden.

She sat down on the blue silk brocade sofa and accepted the cup Mrs Telford handed her.

'How do you think he's looking?'

'Marvellous,' said Cathy, smiling.

'I'm not sure,' Mrs. Telford sighed. 'I think he's pushing himself too fast—he gets so tired, he's trying to rush things. He could have a setback if

he drives himself so hard, but he won't listen to me.'
She looked at Cathy half pleadingly, half angrily.
'But he'll listen to you, Cathy, I want you to talk to
him, get him to see the risk he's running.'

'Have you talked to Dr Plummer?'

Mrs Telford nodded, her mouth a thin line.

'What did he say?'

'He was very cautious, he always is—he told me
to keep a watching brief, whatever that means.
I suppose he wants to wait until Stephen collap-
ses before he puts a halt to all this struggle. Day
after day Stephen forces himself out of that chair
and I can't bear to watch him killing himself just
to . . .'

'Walk again?' Cathy cut in quietly. 'It's
understandable that he wants to walk again—you
don't want him sitting in a wheelchair for the rest
of his life, do you?'

'Of course I don't! But I want him alive, in or
out of a wheelchair. I'm afraid of the strain all this
is putting on his heart. Sometimes he looks grey,
he looks so old, I can't stand it!' There was
anguish in the older woman's voice, in her face,
and hostility in her eyes as she looked at Cathy.
'He's determined to walk because you won't marry
him until he can . . .'

Cathy took a fierce, hurt breath. 'That isn't true!
I'd marry him tomorrow, I've told him that—it's
Stephen who insists on waiting.'

'Because he knows you'll never feel married
until he's on his own two feet—he told me so,' Mrs
Telford burst out in a tone that held bitterness,
and Cathy whitened.

'No, I never said . . .'

'You didn't have to—do you think my son doesn't feel what you're feeling?'

'I'm not ...' Cathy began, and stopped as the doorbell rang. Mrs Telford turned her head, listening, frowning.

'Who on earth can that be at this hour?' She looked at her watch. 'It's gone ten!'

'I'll go,' said Cathy, Nandy was upstairs in her own room, which was next door to Stephen's, she would not answer the doorbell. Cathy crossed the hall and opened the front door, staring in blank astonishment at two policemen who stood outside.

'Evening, miss, sorry to disturb you,' one of them said, swinging a heavy rubber torch in one hand. 'We've had a report that a man has been seen lurking in your garden ...'

'In the garden?' Cathy echoed, alarm in her eyes. 'When?'

'A short time ago, miss—a motorist who was driving along the main road saw a figure in the shrubs near your gate.' Turning, the young man shone his torch across the lawn, picking out the mass of dark laurels near the high iron gates. 'Over there, I suppose—we just took a look, but we didn't see anyone. Would you mind if we search the gardens? Have you heard any unusual noises, seen anything yourself?'

'No, I don't think so,' said Cathy, turning as Mrs Telford came slowly towards them across the hall. 'Mrs Telford, it seems ...'

'I know, I heard.' Mrs Telford looked at the two men, her brows drawn. 'By all means search the gardens. We'll look through the house.'

'It's a big house,' the policeman with the torch said doubtfully. 'Maybe you should let us do that, madam—if there was anyone hiding in one of the rooms you could get hurt. Why don't you and the young lady go back into the room there and we'll take a look for you?'

'Thank you,' said Mrs Telford, stepping back.

Cathy was thinking. 'Could we see your identification, please?' she asked as the two men stepped into the house. They might be wearing police uniform, but it seemed wise to make quite certain that they were genuine.

The man with the torch gave her a smile. 'Certainly, miss,' he said, fishing a card out of his pocket and handing it to her. Cathy read it carefully, then gave it back to him.

'Sorry, I just wanted to make sure . . .'

'Very sensible, miss—I'll start looking on the ground floor; Harry, you take the upstairs rooms.' He smiled at Cathy. 'Perhaps you'd like to come with one of us to show us around, miss?'

'I think that's an excellent idea,' Mrs Telford said briskly, having recovered from her temporary alarm. 'Cathy, you show this officer around, I'll take the other young man through the rest of the house.'

They searched the house thoroughly, checking all the windows, looking into cupboards and under beds, but there was no sign of an entry and no sign of anything stolen. The police spent half an hour in the gardens, the gleam of their torch visible in the darkness and the crunch of their feet and their voices coming up to the house quite clearly. Stephen woke up and Cathy went in to explain what was happening.

'A false alarm, obviously,' she said. 'It must be this scare that's all over Westoak, people are seeing lurking figures everywhere.'

The police took the same view when they called at the house before driving away. 'Sorry to have disturbed you,' they said. 'We didn't find any sign that someone had been in the garden—but if you do hear or see anything, call the station at once.'

When they had gone, Cathy suggested that she should stay the night. 'I don't like the idea of leaving you all alone here,' she said.

Mrs Telford accepted the offer gratefully and Cathy rang her father to warn him that she would not be home that night.

She spent the night in a room looking out over the front garden, but slept badly; and kept hearing sounds, waking from a light sleep to listen tensely. She had breakfast with Mrs Telford at eight, went up to say hello to Stephen and kiss him before they drove off to the office and felt distinctly one degree under as she followed Mrs Telford's car out of the open gates. She parked her own car in the firm's car park and walked into the building in time to join Jennie at the lift. Jennie always came into Westoak with her father, who worked nearby.

'We had some excitement last night,' Cathy said, and told Jennie what had happened. Jennie listened, her dark eyes wide.

'How scary! I wonder if anyone was there?'

'I doubt it, but if there was, he was frightened off when the police arrived.'

She had a very busy day ahead of her. Mrs Telford was having lengthy negotiations with a firm of architects who were going to design the latest hotel in the chain, and Jennie and Cathy were brought in on the discussions that morning. After lunch Cathy had to sit in on a meeting to discuss the interior decor of the York hotel.

Her father was having dinner with friends that evening. Cathy drove straight to Garth House and spent an hour with Stephen. He was tired, rather pale, after all the alarm of the previous evening, and she left him at eight o'clock to drive home, intending to get an early night herself. When she parked outside the little cottage the windows were dark. Cathy walked up the path, feeling oddly nervous, wishing her father was not out. It was stupid, but she was reluctant, suddenly, to go into the empty house. The garden breathed around her, full of night sounds; rustlings and scratchings, the noise of the trees bending in the wind, the whisper of the leaves.

Her hand shook as she inserted the key in the lock. She pushed open the door, listening to the silence, and fumbled for the light switch.

The light came on, and she stood on the threshold, hesitating. She couldn't hear a sound. The house was obviously empty, it was silly to feel nervous, but she could not get out of her head a strange feeling that someone was watching her, someone was hiding in the darkness at the top of the house. The back of her neck was prickling with alarm and she couldn't bring herself to go into the house.

When a movement came, though, it came from behind her. She turned hurriedly with a stifled cry, but she was too late. A man's hand clamped down over her mouth and she was shoved through the front door, struggling but helpless.

CHAPTER THREE

IN a state of mindless panic, Cathy writhed and kicked, trying to bite the hand over her mouth, aware all the time that there was another hand just below her breast, pushed hard against the soft warmth of her flesh. She could hear the man breathing, feel the power of his body. She didn't need to see his face to know that he was dangerous, she felt it, it emanated from him in waves. His hands were brutal: they were hurting her, and they meant to, their cruel grasp was deliberate.

The front door slammed behind them as he kicked it shut. With a final violent struggle, Cathy broke free, then her arm was grabbed and she was whirled to face him.

Shock hit her in the face as she recognised him. 'Muir!' Her heart missed a beat, the breath was forced out of her lungs in a painful contraction.

He let go of her and she backed, her terrified eyes fixed on his face. He looked different; a black leather jacket emphasising the muscled width of his shoulders, dark jeans making him look taller, tougher. The man she had fallen in love with in Nice had been warm and charming—this man facing her was a very different proposition.

'Surprised to see me?' he asked, his features harsh and implacable, and she watched his mouth twist in a bitter derision. 'What's the matter,

Cathy? You look quite scared, but then you have good reason to be, haven't you?'

Moistening her lips, she whispered dryly: 'What are you doing here?'

The grey eyes which had once held such charm when he looked at her, now held a chilling contempt; a remorseless probe which lanced her white face, as if he saw the fear in it with a grim satisfaction.

'I thought it was time one of your little games blew up in your face,' he said. 'Girls who play with dangerous toys have to be taught a lesson.' He walked towards her and Cathy backed, her legs trembling under her, trying to get control of herself so that she could talk to him without her voice giving out on her, as she knew it would if she tried to speak at the moment. Her throat felt raw and dry, there were tears burning behind her lids. If she tried to speak she knew those tears would betray her, would let him know how much it hurt her to have him talking to her in that voice, feel his hard grey eyes flicking over her as though he hated the sight of her.

She found herself in the dark sitting-room and stopped, biting her lip. Muir switched on the light and threw a swift glance around the room. Cathy seized on the moment, while his attention was elsewhere, to pull herself together. When she first saw him, she had been so disturbed that she had had the crazy idea that Muir was the man who had been terrorising the town, but of course he wasn't, and some of the fear leaked out of her as she dismissed that idea. If she hadn't been so shaken such a thought would never have entered her head.

He looked back at her, lifting one brow. 'You're very quiet. Working out what to do, are you?'

'I wish you hadn't come here, Muir,' she began, and he laughed without humour.

'Oh, I'm sure you do—inconvenient of me not to play your game the way you planned it, isn't it?'

'I didn't plan anything! It just happened.' She saw his cynical smile and sighed. 'Muir, why don't you just forget you ever met me?'

'The way you intend to forget you ever met me?' he asked bitingly, and her pale face ran with colour that washed up to her hair.

'I wish I could!' She stopped dead as the sentence escaped and Muir's eyes narrowed on her with a silvery, thoughtful gleam.

'Is that some sort of backhanded compliment? Aren't you finding me quite as easy to forget as all the others?'

'What others?' she answered blankly, then realised what he had meant, and said wearily: 'There are no others, there never have been—it never happened before. Muir, you've got to believe me.'

'Have I? Why should I? Why on earth should I ever believe a word you say?'

She winced, her neck bending as though the weight of her head was too much for it. She wanted to cry, even more, but she refused to let the tears escape—they would not move Muir, he would sneer at them, and she wouldn't let herself descend to pleading.

'Why are you here?' she asked in a voice so low he had to take a step closer to hear her.

'Why? You left me with a lot of questions to

which there seemed no answers,' he said. 'I'm a reporter—my training made me want to find out what those answers were. I'd have been here sooner if I could have got the time off, but I was sent off to Dublin by the paper when I got back to London, and I've only just managed to wangle some leave.'

'We've got nothing to talk about,' Cathy said desperately. 'I know I behaved badly . . .'

'Oh, you know that, do you?' He gave her a grim smile and she winced.

'You despise me and I deserve it, but this isn't doing any good.'

Muir stripped off his black leather jacket and slung it over a chair, raking back his thick hair as it tumbled across his forehead. 'Give me the answers to my questions, then I'll go.' He looked around the small sitting-room, his brows lifted. 'I prefer this house to the monstrosity the Telfords live in . . .'

'Garth House?' Cathy stared at him, her lips parted in shock. 'You . . . you haven't been there? You haven't talked to Stephen?'

He threw her a hard, sardonic smile. 'You can stop shaking like a leaf. I didn't talk to anyone. I just took a look around the house.'

'This afternoon?'

'Last night after dinner,' he said. 'I walked a little way up the drive and saw the house.' His face was cold as he surveyed her. 'I saw you, too—looking out of an upstairs window. Who was that with you? Telford? I thought for a minute you had heard me moving about, I saw the faces staring out and got behind one of the bushes.' The grey eyes stabbed at her in sudden, fierce contempt. 'I watched him kiss you. It didn't look like whirlwind passion to me, or is he the slow-burning sort? Is that why you've been engaged for two years? Why you have little flings with other men?'

Cathy was not listening. 'You were there last night? What time?'

'Who knows?' Muir said impatiently, then shrugged. 'Oh, around ten, I suppose.'

She stared at him, her lips parting on a gasp of shock. 'That was you?'

'You saw me?' Muir's eyes fixed on her face, his brows drawn.

'I didn't, but a motorist saw you as he drove past the gates; he rang the police and a patrol car came along, they searched the house and gardens.' Cathy was pale and trembling, her imagination working overtime. 'Why did you do it? Muir! If you'd been caught . . .'

'Yes, that could have been awkward for you, couldn't it?' he mocked. 'It could have blown your little world sky-high.'

She flinched from the bitter hostility in his face. 'Muir, you don't understand . . .'

'I understand one thing,' he said in a barely controlled voice, and her senses leapt in alarm as he fastened his fingers into her shoulders and drew her towards him. Cathy opened her mouth to protest, then found herself staring into the dark grey eyes, seeing the leaping violence in them with an answering emotion.

'Your body talks to mine,' said Muir, shaking her to emphasise the words. 'Every time we're together I'm aware of it, You can't hide it from me, whatever else you've hidden, some things don't need words.'

'Don't, Muir,' she whispered, trembling, then his right hand slipped slowly down her arm to the strained tension of her breast, and the shock of his touch made her breath catch in a shuddered pleasure. Her eyes half-closed, her body arched of its own accord in an involuntary movement, seeking the contact with his which she needed so desperately, and Muir's breathing quickened, his arm went round her and held her fiercely as his mouth found hers. Cathy's arms went round his neck and she kissed him back with something like desperation.

He had scarcely been out of her thoughts since she last saw him. She had been dying to see him again, and now he was holding her, kissing her as though he felt exactly the same way.

He lifted his head slowly a moment later and her face remained lifted, her eyes closed and her lips parted moistly, silently begging for him to kiss her again.

'Either you're the world's best actress since Garbo, or you feel about me the same way I feel about you,' Muir said huskily. 'Which is it, Cathy?'

Reluctantly she opened her eyes, their green depths misty, drowsy with passion. 'I wish you hadn't come,' she whispered, her mouth shaking.

'Do you do this all the time? How many others have you snared like this?' Muir asked in biting contempt, and she flinched.

'Muir, two years ago Stephen crashed his car. He was almost killed. It was months before we could even hope he would live—his injuries were appalling. He had months of plastic surgery before he came home and the doctors said he would never walk again. He was totally paralysed.'

Muir had frozen as she started to talk, but his arm had tightened around her and she saw from his unsmiling face that he was listening intently. The contempt had died out of his eyes, they were grim and very dark.

'Two years is a long, long time,' Cathy went on. 'I don't know how long it was before I realised I didn't love him any more, but can you imagine how much I hated myself when I realised that? I wouldn't think about it, I told myself I still cared enough about him to be happy with him after we were married. I thought that once Stephen could walk again I'd start feeling the way I always used to—I refused to face up to it. I made myself take each day as it came. The only thing that mattered was to keep Stephen happy. He has such tremendous will power—although the doctors said he might never walk again he's never given up believing that he will. It was an effort for him just to sit up at first.'

'Last night,' Muir broke in, frowning. 'Wasn't that Telford with you at the window, then?'

'Yes, that was Stephen. He's walking now, but he has to have a stick and it still tires him. He can only walk short distances so far.'

Muir let go of her and walked away. She watched him uncertainly; his tense face and contracted brows showed that he did believe her. He paced to and fro, his eyes on the floor, then swung towards her.

'How long do you think it will be before he's back to normal?'

'I don't know, none of us do. He's still very weak, he gets depressed at times. His progress is often two steps forward, one step back. It takes a lot of courage for him to keep fighting.'

'I'm sorry,' Muir said flatly. 'He's had a tough deal, poor guy. I'd hate to be bedridden, it would drive me crazy.'

She smiled at him with tenderness, amused. 'Yes.' She could imagine that—Muir was far too fiercely energetic to find it easy to bear long confinement to one room.

'All the same,' he said, watching that smile. 'All the same, Cathy, however tough a deal Telford has had, you can't marry him and you know it.'

The smile vanished and her face tightened. 'You don't understand—when he was paralysed he had to fix an idea in his head, a goal to work towards. He said he wouldn't get married until he could walk without a stick, and he's stuck to that ever since.' She looked at him pleadingly, her lashes damp. 'I couldn't leave him. He might stop trying. Once, when he was very ill, he told me he sometimes thought of killing himself . . .'

Muir halted in front of her, anger blazing out of his eyes. 'My God, that's emotional blackmail of a pretty low sort!'

'Don't talk like that, Muir,' Cathy stammered, her lower lip quivering with pain. 'Not about Stephen—if you knew him, you wouldn't suspect anything of the sort.' She felt very tired, she leaned her face against him, her cheek against the hard bone structure of that very masculine face. His strength seemed to seep into her as she moved her cheek gently against his, feeling the faint prickle of the tiny hairs along his jaw. 'You need a shave,' she whispered, smiling.

'Do I?' Muir took two steps backward, holding her, taking her with him, and sat down in a chair, pulling Cathy on to his lap. Her head lay against his shoulder, her body relaxed with his arm around her waist. He looked down at her through his flicking lashes, smiling.

'I love you, Cathy.'

Her stomach plunged in weak tenderness. She put a hand up to his face, stroking his cheek. 'Muir,' she whispered.

'Say it, darling,' he said in low, roughened tones. 'Say it—I can see it in your eyes, but I want to hear it.'

'I've no right to,' she said unhappily, her face slowly flushing as she met those grey eyes and saw the fire in them leap up like a fed furnace, scorching her with the intensity of his demand for her love.

'Why do you think I'm here?' he asked, his arm tightening on her. 'I couldn't let you go. I was bloody mad at first, that night you told me about Telford. I meant to fly home and forget I ever saw you—I hated you. I'd fallen for you hook, line and sinker on the plane, the first day we met, and I'd been so sure you felt the same way.' He looked at her, his eyes half closed, breathing thickly, then bent and let his lips run along the soft, gentle curve of her cheek, the lightness of the kiss barely stirring the tiny golden hairs which were almost invisibly present on her smooth skin. Cathy's body trembled, she felt her heart hammering in her throat.

'I haven't any family, Cathy,' Muir said roughly. 'I was an only child, my parents died a few years back. I've kept moving all my life, in my job it pays to travel light. I've worked all over the world; the States, Australia, the Far East. I've been everywhere, done everything—but I'm thirty-six and the world's a very small place and getting smaller by the hour. I'm lonely and my life's empty—it has been for a long time. You say Telford needs you? Cathy, he couldn't need you the way I do.'

She looked at him in shock, taken aback by what he had said. The way they had met in Nice had shown her a clever, sophisticated man with a strong sense of humour and a quick-witted cynicism about life. Forceful, energetic, Muir had seemed to be a natural loner, a man who met life with his teeth bared and forced it to give him what he wanted. Cathy had not expected him to reveal this very different side of himself.

He looked down at her restlessly, frowning as though angry that he had revealed so much. 'We've got something special, Cathy, don't throw it away.'

'Can't you see how hard this is for me?' she said shakily. 'Stephen . . .'

'You don't love him, Cathy—do you? Okay, you're very fond of the poor guy, but you aren't in love with him, are you?' Muir had hard certainty in his eyes as he forced her to meet them, held her chin tipped up so that she had to look at him.

Her body shivered in a hopeless sigh. 'No,' she said huskily, 'I'm not in love with him.'

Muir smiled brilliantly, his eyes tender in

triumph. 'And you are in love with me, aren't you, darling?'

Her lips parted, trembled, the word was formed, but no sound escaped, and Muir smiled, putting one long finger on her mouth to feel the word. 'Say it, Cathy, let me hear it.'

'I love you,' she whispered then, and was suddenly so tired she closed her eyes and let her body slacken against him. Muir didn't speak, or move, he just held her, his cheek against her hair, and the body warmth flowed between them into a tender poise of love; like a seesaw balanced perfectly with neither of them up or down, but meeting on one plane.

It was several minutes before Muir said: 'Do you want me to come with you to tell Telford?'

'I can't tell him, Muir,' she protested. 'He's too ill!'

'You've got to—if he has guts he'll be tough enough to take the truth. You don't want to marry him any more, he's got to be told that.'

'If anything happened because I walked out on him I'd never forgive myself, don't you see that?'

'When will you tell him, then?' Muir shifted and looked into her distressed eyes. 'You do intend to tell him sooner or later, don't you? How long is it going to drag on?'

'I can't fix a date like someone making an appointment with a dentist! How do I know when Stephen will be strong enough . . .'

'A month? Three? How long?' Muir insisted, frowning. 'And what about me? You don't expect me to go away and wait in London until you do get around to telling him? I've got to see you,

Cathy—how are we going to manage that in a town this size without someone seeing us together and starting gossip?'

Cathy looked desperately around the familiar little sitting-room; her eye dwelling on the walnut-cased clock on the mantelshelf, the stereo equipment which her father cherished, the paintings on the wall, some of which had been painted by ex-pupils from the school. All those personal belongings, the background to her whole life, meant nothing, gave her no sense of security as she realised the bitter extent of her problem.

'You're not sending me away again, Cathy,' Muir said deeply. 'You're mine, and I'm not being locked out of your life until you can get up the nerve to tell Telford the truth. I'll wait until you think he's well enough to be told—but I'm not going away again, you've got to promise we'll see each other.'

She looked ahead into a future strewn with thorns—if they did meet it would have to be secretly, how could she possibly get away very often? She had to be at Garth House every day or Stephen would start asking questions, and if Muir came to Westoak to see her, sooner or later someone would be bound to see them. He was right about that. Gossip spread in this town like wildfire.

She was ice-cold, but she knew what she had to say. 'I can't do it, Muir,' she said, dry-mouthed. 'It wouldn't work—I'd hate living a lie . . .'

'What else do you live now?' he broke out harshly, and she shrank.

'That's different!'

'You're not sending me away!' Muir muttered in hoarse determination, his arms closing around her, then he got up, carrying her, and in a stab of alarm Cathy looked up at the strong-boned face just a few inches above her.

'What are you doing?' He shifted her weight, his arms tightening, and walked across the room without answering. 'Muir! Muir, put me down!' Cathy protested urgently, beginning to struggle, her anxiety growing.

He halted at the foot of the stairs and looked down at her, then kissed her with almost brutal insistence; the pressure of his mouth lingering with a cruelty that suffocated her moans of protest, forced her lips to part and demanded a total submission before he lifted his head again, leaving Cathy lying, half fainting, her body boneless in his arms.

Without another word he began to climb the stairs, his breathing rapid and thick. Cathy's head lay back against the strong arm supporting it, she felt her head spinning, she was dizzy and sick with an explosive mixture of fear and a desire she hadn't expected. All the sensual passion she had locked away inside her for the past two years had come leaping to the surface as Muir kissed her; smashing through the inhibitions her mind placed on her feelings, as though the sheer ferocity of that kiss had ripped away every barrier between them, shown her that she needed his cruelty as much as she needed the coaxing persuasion of his caressing fingers because the depth of the emotion between them demanded such intense expression.

Muir halted on the landing and looked about

him at the bedroom doors, then walked towards the one which was open. His eyes pierced the shadows to find the dressing-table on which Cathy's perfume and make-up were neatly arranged, then he walked over to the bed and put her down.

She had begun to pull herself together shivering. 'Muir, no—I'm not going to let you . . . '

He hadn't put on the light, he stood there in the darkness staring at her, and she heard him unbuttoning his shirt, heard the rasp of his nail on the material. Her nerves jumped sickeningly. She tensed, staring at him, shrinking back, like a frightened cat, green eyes all dilated pupil, the hair stirring on the back of her neck.

He flung his shirt towards a chair and she heard him unzip his jeans. With a cry of fear Cathy leapt off the bed, wriggled to evade his reaching arm and ran towards the door.

Muir muttered a brief obscenity. He flung his jeans on to the chair and came after her. Their bodies collided at the top of the stairs, his fingers clamped on her shirt and it ripped as she tripped and fell. Muir came down with her, his hands closing over her wrists as she twisted to escape him.

'I won't sleep with you,' Cathy whispered. 'Muir, do you hear me? Let me go, this is crazy, what do you think I am? Why are you doing this?'

'Because you're mine and I'm not walking away leaving you to marry a man you aren't in love with,' Muir said breathlessly, then his mouth took hers and she whimpered under the force of the kiss. His hands touched her body with a delicacy

and fire she found painful, she moaned, her hands
holding his dark head, trying to thrust him away.
Muir had unzipped her skirt, she felt him dragging
it down and her fingers dug into the side of his
face in a reflex of fear, she felt her nails sink into
his flesh, and he swore again. Cathy tried to roll
away, but he dragged her back, anchored her
under him with the weight of his body. He had
taken off her skirt in the brief struggle and tossed
it away. She heard it rustle down the stairs in the
darkness.

'You're mad, you can't do this!' she gasped.
'You're hurting, Muir! I don't want to, don't make
me—please, Muir, for God's sake, not like this!'

His face was buried between her breasts, she felt
the warmth of his breath on her cold skin, his
parted lips against her nipple, and her body arched
in agonising pleasure even while she protested, as
if she had divided into two; her mind at war with
her body, the one denying, the other clamouring
for what he was doing. Angrily she began to fight
in earnest, hating herself because half of her
wanted him to take her and Muir could sense it,
she couldn't hide it from him, the taut arch of her
body telling him what she did not want him to
know.

She had no hope of winning their struggle;
biting, scratching, twisting, she was finally pinned
to the floor and held there by cruel hands, her
body heaving in breathless defeat. Muir pinioned
her beneath him, his breathing thick, and she
looked up to see his eyes gleaming in the darkness.

'I need you,' he said unevenly, the sound like a
groan. 'I want you so much I've been going slowly

insane these past weeks. Stop fighting it, Cathy, admit you want me too.'

Wearily, she let her lids fall, her body lapsing into weak submission, and Muir took a long, deep breath.

'Cathy,' he muttered, his lips grazing hungrily along her neck, and she felt his fingertips stroking the inside of her thighs. Cathy moaned and put her free arm around his body, holding him as though she was drowning and had no other hope of survival, in a desperate, yearning embrace. As he took her, a wild cry broke out of her, and Muir kissed her, his hand cupping her breast, sensuously brushing his thumb across her nipple.

Now that she had stopped fighting she was aching with aroused desire, her hands running along the smooth indentation of his spine, feeling the tiny hairs along it prickling her palms. She stroked the cool skin stretching those powerful shoulders, the taut muscles of his neck, and pressed her face into his throat, her lips apart, the moistness of her mouth heated as she kissed his neck and felt the pulse of his blood quickening.

She had been refusing to think of this bitter frustration, she had not allowed herself to admit how she felt, what she needed, but once she gave in to the nagging imperative of a desire for satisfaction, the driving necessity took control.

Tomorrow she might bitterly regret that she had let this happen, but now, tonight, she surrendered to the slow-building intensity that spiralled inside her with every movement, until her voice seemed to break through the very top of her head in fierce cries.

Afterwards Muir rolled away and lay on his back, breathing as though he was dying, each breath harshly drawn, his body shuddering.

Cathy didn't move, her eyes fixed on the darkness above her. She felt her body growing cold, her mind even colder. From under her lids crawled the slow tears. She swallowed on salt, and forced herself to move, to get up. Muir got up, too, and caught her arm, staring down at her fixedly.

'Don't,' he said. 'Don't cry, I didn't mean to hurt you, Cathy, but you made me go mad—it would kill me to think of you marrying him, don't you realise that? You say it would kill him if you left—what about me? I'm the man you love, not him, you've admitted it—you can't marry him, live with him, feeling like that about me. It would be despicable . . . '

'You're the one who's despicable,' she broke out bitterly. 'You made me do that—you had no right! How could you . . .'

'You wanted me,' Muir said harshly, his eyes a brilliant stab of light as he stared down at her. 'You can't deny it.'

'You forced me to make love to you, I hated it!' Cathy shouted, hating herself so much she felt she hated him, she wanted to hurt him the way she was hurt.

Muir's hand pushed her away, she fell backwards with a cry of terror and heard him gasp: 'Cathy! No . . .'

She couldn't recover her balance, she clutched wildly at the wooden rail along the side of the stairs, but her perspiring palms were too slippery, they would not hold, she was falling, crashing, her body tumbling over and over, her head smashing against the wall one minute and the next hitting the floor with an impact that made every bone in her body jar in agony. She lay there, whimpering, her mouth full of the taste of pain.

Someone bent over her, there was movement blurring in front of her clouding eyes.

'Cathy! My God, Cathy, what's he done to you?'

She had to struggle hard to hold back the darkness and she could barely see the white glare of the face, but she recognised her father's appalled voice and shame and misery washed over her.

'I didn't want to do it, Daddy,' she whispered in a weak, thready voice. 'He made me, he hurt me. I couldn't help it!'

CHAPTER FOUR

SHE woke up feeling as though her head was stuffed with cotton wool; she was dull, grey, remote from everything around her. Even the sounds in the ward seemed to come from far away; she seemed to hear them through a defective radio, they came and went, buzzing and crackling in her ears. Faces swam out of the mist around her, their mouths opened, and Cathy stared at them as the lips moved, but she couldn't quite hear what they were saying, so most of the time she just closed her eyes after a moment. She didn't try to answer them—she didn't feel they were really there. None of it made sense, but she was too tired to think about that.

She was in a little cubicle at the end of the ward, and there was a cream-painted partition at one side of her bed. Against it sat someone who rarely moved. Cathy knew he was there, she saw him out of the corner of her eye, but she never looked at him because he frightened her, she wasn't sure why. He was a dark blue shape, she heard him breathing, coughing now and then, shifting his feet, moving on his chair so that the legs squeaked. Whenever anyone came into the cubicle he sat up. If they came over to the bed and spoke to Cathy he got up and stood behind them. Cathy pretended she didn't see him, but she soon got to know his face, it was long and flat and serious, a pale slab out of which blue eyes watched her alertly.

Once when she opened her eyes he was standing by her bed, watching her. Cathy shrank against the pillows, frowning, and it hurt to frown, her head hurt. She put a shaky hand up to it. There were bandages swathing it, she felt them, and the man in the blue uniform bent down and spoke to her.

'Miss Winter?' He paused, watching Cathy as if waiting for her to answer, and when she was silent, he said: 'How do you feel, miss? I'm a police officer.'

Cathy shut her eyes again, but he didn't vanish, as he had before when he had said that, the cotton wool no longer seemed so thick, it did not protect her from him this time.

'I have to ask you a few questions, miss,' he went on, and as Cathy's face quivered added quickly: 'Nothing to be worried about.' He bent closer. 'Could you tell me what happened? Last night, Miss Winter, what happened?'

There was a rustle and the affronted slap of flat-soled shoes on a rubber floor, then a brisk voice said: 'Please sit down, Constable. I told you, there's no point in trying to question her yet. She's under sedation and anything she said would be sheer nonsense. If you don't sit down and keep out of our way you'll have to go and sit in the corridor.'

'Sorry, Sister,' he said meekly, and slunk back to his chair. Cathy sank into a dull state between sleep and waking, and when she opened her eyes again she found a man in a white coat holding her wrist between finger and thumb. He wasn't looking at her, he was gazing vacantly ahead, humming under his breath.

He replaced her hand on the cool white cover, looking down at her as he did so, and saw Cathy's eyes open. He smiled. 'Well, hello there, how are you? Feeling any better now? Head okay?'

'What have I done to my head?' Cathy asked, and heard a movement. Over his shoulder she saw the slab-like face.

'You were silly enough to fall on it,' the doctor told her, glancing sideways. 'You've got a fan here, Miss Winter, he's dying to ask you some questions about yourself. Do you feel up to answering them?'

'I suppose so,' Cathy said reluctantly, because she couldn't think of a way of refusing, although she wasn't even sure why she felt so unwilling to talk to the policeman. 'But I don't remember how I hurt myself—I've been trying to think, but . . .' She broke off, staring at the doctor. 'Did I crash the car?'

The two men stared down at her. The doctor looked at the policeman, his brows lifting. The policeman chewed on his lower lip, his face blank.

Cathy looked at him nervously. 'I . . . didn't hurt anyone, did I?' She was afraid, her skin icy— why else had he been sitting there, waiting for her to talk to him? She must have crashed the car and injured someone—killed them, had she killed someone? She swallowed painfully, trembling. 'What have I done?' she whispered, wrenched with fear. 'What have I done?' She couldn't remember whatever had happened, but she felt the dead weight of guilt falling on her, her stomach

clenched in sick misery. She knew, somewhere at
the back of her mind, that she had done something
terrible, she was afraid and ashamed and hated
herself. She didn't want to think about herself,
self-loathing was twisting inside her.

The doctor answered. He waved the policeman
away and smiled at Cathy. 'No, you didn't crash
your car and you didn't hurt anyone, Miss Winter.
Now, stop worrying. There's nothing to be
worried about, you haven't done anything.' He
moved back and she heard him whispering to the
thin, silent Sister in her white uniform, her severely
capped head just on the periphery of Cathy's
vision, then Cathy heard the squeak of the
policeman's shoes as he walked away. They all
went away. Cathy lay there, searching her mind.
What had happened, then? She hadn't crashed her
car? What had happened?

Later that day her father arrived with a large
bunch of roses. Cathy smiled at him, 'Oh, lovely!'
They were fat pink roses with dusty yellow hearts.
Her father laid them on the bedside table and
pollen drifted upwards in the sunny air. He pulled
up a chair and sat down on it.

'How do you feel?' he asked, but he didn't look
at her, his eyes slid away before they reached her
face, and Cathy felt his reluctance, it hurt her.

He asked: 'Is there anything you want: I'll bring
some fruit tomorrow, can I bring you a nightie or
something?' His voice was careful and polite, but
Cathy heard the distance in it—her father couldn't
look at her, there was an embarrassd flush on his
face—what was he thinking? What had she done to
make her father so unwilling even to meet her eyes?

'How's school?' she asked, because it made a neutral subject, and he always liked talking about his job.

She heard the note of relief with which he started telling her about the row he was having with some of the teachers about discipline. George Winter took an old-fashioned attitude to it, he disliked the modern theories about children. He was a stern disciplinarian himself, he believed that to spare the rod spoiled the child. He had never slapped Cathy as a little girl, he had left her discipline to her mother, but if she made too much noise or did something naughty her father would look at her coldly, frowning, and she would shrink into a stiff little ramrod before sidling out of his sight.

That was how she felt now, she was relieved when he left. The policeman had not come back, and she wondered if they'd put him in the corridor, but the nurses laughed when she asked them. 'No, he's gone,' they said, but although they were lighthearted as they made her bed, plumped up her pillows, gave her a pill and a glass of water, even they were oddly on guard with her. She couldn't even put her finger on what she felt about their attitude. They were very kind, they smiled, but there was still a barrier there.

A few hours later Stephen visited her. Cathy had her eyes shut, her head back against the pillows, when she heard the door open. She looked towards it and felt herself shrink inwardly as he came through the door, leaning heavily on his stick, breathing audibly after having walked from the main door of the hospital.

He stood there, staring at her, his face pale, a strangely drawn look on it. 'How are you?' His voice sounded husky, she got the feeling he was as uneasy as everyone else she had seen, but at least he looked at her, his eyes searched her face.

'Bruised all over,' she said, trying to smile, and saw Stephen flinch. Cathy's eyes widened and she began to feel even more anxious. 'Don't stand, it will tire you,' she said quickly. 'Come and sit down, darling.'

Stephen limped over towards her and lowered himself on to the chair, propping his stick over the back of it. 'I brought you some books and some flowers,' he said. 'Mother will bring them in later.'

'Did she drive you?' Cathy was surprised. Nandy usually drove him when he went out.

He nodded. 'She wanted to see you.'

'That was nice of her.' Cathy looked down and began to pleat the white coverlet with shaky fingers. 'Did they tell you I've got amnesia? Isn't it weird? I can't remember anything that happened and they won't tell me. You'll tell me, won't you, Stephen? What have I done? I know something's wrong, I can feel it. I've got to know or I'll go crazy!'

Stephen made an inaudible sound and put a hand over the restless fingers, his skin warm against hers. 'Cathy,' he said deeply, 'you haven't done anything—stop it.'

'I've got to know, Stephen—you don't understand, it's driving me crazy not to know, don't hide it from me!'

'The only thing you have to think about is getting well, don't dwell on . . .'

'How can I help it? I can't remember what happened and nobody will tell me—they won't even talk about it. My father came and he just sat there, he couldn't even bear to look at me!'

Stephen frowned, his eyes shining as though there were a film of tears over them, then he looked away from her, his mouth unsteady. 'You're imagining things. Your father has always been very quiet.'

'He's ashamed of me,' she whispered miserably, close to tears.

'Cathy! Of course he isn't! Why on earth should he be? You haven't got a thing to blame yourself for—nobody's blaming you.' His hand clenched over hers, he moved violently in his chair, she felt tension vibrating inside him and looked at him anxiously. 'I'd like to get my hands . . .' he began, then as he saw her face he cut the words off. After a long moment he said flatly: 'All you have to think about is getting well, don't lie here worrying about . . . about anything.'

She watched him, wishing she could read his mind. He was angry—she felt that as strongly as if he had hit her, yet that anger didn't seem to be directed towards her. His illness had altered his character more than she had ever imagined it would. Before the crash, Stephen had been lively, busy, great fun to be with—the long months of pain had made him thoughtful, quiet, a man so used to living inside himself that he hid far more than he revealed. He had acquired a new patience, a deeper tenacity. It was a long time since Cathy had seen him so worked up about anything.

She didn't want him to be upset, she twined her

fingers around his and managed to smile at him. 'Sorry, darling, I'm only being stupid. Forgive me?' She used a light tone, but his face did not relax. If anything, it tightened. She heard the unsteady breath he took, then he lifted her hand to his lips and kissed it, his head bent so that she couldn't see his face.

'Nothing to forgive,' he muttered against her skin, then looked up and asked: 'Is the food here as bad as ever?'

Cathy managed to laugh. 'I've only had one meal, and that wasn't bad. I'd forgotten how many months you spent in here . . .'

'I hadn't,' Stephen said drily, and she looked at him with apology.

'Of course you wouldn't—sorry, darling.'

'Don't keep apologising,' Stephen said tersely, and she flinched. 'Sorry, Cathy,' he said on a tired note.

Mrs Telford appeared in the doorway as Cathy was looking at him, her eyes nervous, and Stephen groped for his stick. 'Time I made way, is it?' he asked, and Cathy distinctly heard a note of relief in his voice. He got to his feet, leaning on his stick, and bent over to kiss her cheek. 'Look after yourself,' he whispered. 'I'll see you tomorrow.'

As he made his way to the door, his mother watched him, frowning. 'I won't be long,' she said, and Stephen nodded.

Mrs Telford came over to the bed, holding a large cellophane-wrapped bouquet of flowers and a couple of thin paperbacks. 'Where shall I put these? On the table?' She carefully put them down, hazel eyes sliding to flick at Cathy and then moving away again. It was beginning to be familiar, that uneasy look. Everyone who came in here seemed to wear it, they seemed both curious and nervous—but why?

'How do you feel? Anything I can get you? We're missing you at the office, I don't know how I'm going to manage without my right hand.' Mrs Telford was rather better at hiding things than Stephen, she talked quickly and lightly, even if she was avoiding Cathy's eyes.

'I'll be back soon,' Cathy said, and Mrs Telford nodded and smiled.

'Of course you will. There's no hurry, we can cope. Carol has offered to fill in for you as much as she can.'

'How kind of her,' Cathy said drily, not a bit surprised to hear that. Carol would be delighted, the understudy would simply leap into the star's shoes, it was her big chance to show that she could do Cathy's job.

Mrs Telford was no fool. She gave Cathy a quick, smiling look. 'Carol's a bright girl, but she doesn't have your brains. I'll be glad to have you back, Cathy, I rely on you. But work must go on, we have a business to run.'

And nobody is indispensable, Cathy thought wryly, understanding her perfectly. Mrs Telford was a shrewd businesswoman; Cathy admired her for the way she had taken over running the firm after her husband died and she valued her good opinion. It was very typical that Mrs Telford should say briskly: work must go on.

Mrs Telford's own life had been marked by a series of emotional blows—the deaths of her husband and favourite son, Stephen's car crash and his long illness. Mrs Telford had taken them all in her stride, forced herself to go on with living, although Cathy did not underestimate the grief she had suffered, Cathy had seen her face whenever anyone mentioned David. Under that sensible exterior, Mrs Telford still grieved, she hadn't forgotten David, but she had refused to allow her pain to take over her whole life. She had strength, and Cathy knew how much Stephen had inherited from his mother that ability to face up to what fate has done to you and somehow carry on in spite of it.

Cathy would hate herself if she had done anything to make either Stephen or his mother despise her. She lay silently when Mrs Telford had gone, aching with self-accusing uncertainty. If only she could remember!

Muir Ingram glanced up at the clock ticking quietly on the blue-painted wall above him. Eight o'clock, he thought, and lifted his arm to look at his watch. It said exactly the same time, and as he caught himself performing the little action in that automatic way, he grimaced. He had done that dozens of times today, it was becoming a nervous habit. It was second nature to him to double-check every fact, just as it was second nature to him to keep his head in a tight corner. And this was certainly a tight corner, he mentally acknowledged, frowning.

That had been obvious from the beginning—and his professional training had come shooting to the fore, reminding him of something he had once

been told by an habitual criminal he had
interviewed for the paper after the man had
written a best-selling book on prison life. 'Never
tell the bastards anything,' the man had said. 'Play
it by the book. All I ever admit to is my name and
address, then I scream for my lawyer, and I keep
on screaming until they let me see him.'

Muir had followed the advice instinctively, his
intelligence still sharp even though he was in ice-
cold shock last night. For the first few moments
after Cathy crashed down those stairs, screaming,
he had been out of his mind with fear for her, he
had taken the stairs three at a time, totally
oblivious of the fact that he was stark naked and
not even aware of the front door opening, the
horrified face of the man entering the house. All he
had thought about was Cathy, but even as he ran
towards her, he had been thrust away. George
Winter had hit him before he knew what was
happening and Muir had rocked backwards and
fallen.

'Leave her alone, you swine!' George Winter
had shouted, shaking, then Muir had heard
Cathy's voice a moment later.

'I didn't want to do it, Daddy, he made me . . .'
she had said, crying, and Muir had got to his feet
feeling sick and bitter.

Her father had gone over to the telephone in the
hall and started to dial, his angry eyes on Muir.
'You needn't try to get away,' he had begun, and
Muir had not understood, even then, what
construction the other man had placed on what he
had seen, what Cathy had said. George Winter
had called an ambulance and Muir had turned on

his heel and gone back up the stairs to get some
clothes on, after he had tossed a quilt down to
Cathy's father and said curtly: 'Wrap her in this,
she'll be frozen.' George Winter had stared up the
stairs at him before he picked up the quilt. Muir
had dressed quickly, but as he came down the
stairs he heard the wail of the police siren as the
car screeched towards the house.

The ambulance had arrived almost at the same
time. Cathy had been out cold, she had been
carried off on a stretcher with a young police
constable walking beside it, and Muir had faced
the two detectives who had stayed behind. By then
his mind had begun to work well enough for him
to realise the sort of tricky situation he had been
placed in—and he had decided to play dumb,
refuse to answer questions until he had a
solicitor.

'My name is Muir Ingram, and I want to see a
solicitor,' he had said with all the coolness he
could muster, and had seen the two men look at
each other.

The older of the two, a broad, heavily built man
in his late forties, had lifted his brows and said
wryly: 'We haven't charged you with anything, Mr
Ingram, have we? We just want to ask you a few
questions about what's happened.'

'It was an accident,' Muir had told them. 'She
fell down the stairs by accident, but you can ask
her all about that yourself—as far as I'm
concerned, I'd prefer to see my solicitor before I
talk to you.'

'Why should you want to see a lawyer before
you co-operate with us, Mr Ingram?' the other

man had asked. 'You haven't committed a crime, have you?'

Cathy's father had broken out furiously: 'You know what he's done to her! How can you not know? You saw what...'

'Mr Winter, why don't you go and sit in the car with Sergeant Lucas?' the older of the two detectives had said, his voice calm but insistent.

George Winter had looked as if he was going to argue for a moment, then he had walked out heavily with the other policeman. Muir had stood there, waiting, and the older detective had said: 'While we're on our own, Mr Ingram, is there anything you'd like to tell me, just between the two of us? We'll have to go along to the station so that you can make a formal statement, but it would save a lot of time and trouble for both of us if you were quite frank now.'

'What am I accused of?' Muir had asked, but he had known—Cathy's father had made that quite clear, the loathing in his eyes had left Muir in no doubt as to what he thought had happened.

'You're not being accused of anything, Mr Ingram—all I want is to hear from you what happened.'

'I'll talk to you when I've seen my solicitor, Inspector ... is it Inspector?' Muir had asked, and the other man had looked irritated and shrugged.

'Yes, Inspector Werrell,' he had admitted. 'Look, Mr Ingram, you're obviously an intelligent man, why waste time like this? Why not make this easy for both of us? I work at the station all day. Believe me, you won't enjoy spending hours kicking your heels in an interview room. I'm a very reasonable man, myself, but some of my colleagues get very impatient when people get awkward with them.' He smiled at Muir to show how reasonable he was and Muir regarded him with weary cynicism.

'I'm not being awkward, Inspector. I have the right to stay silent.'

'Oh, rights, is it?' the Inspector had said. 'I see— all right, Mr Ingram, let's go and start the circus.' He had taken Muir's arm and hustled him towards the door, and Muir had known that if he objected, or struggled, he might very well find himself facing an initial charge of resisting arrest, so he had grimly allowed himself to be marched like a criminal down to the waiting police car, and shoved inside.

Cathy's father had been sitting in the front seat. He had looked at Muir once or twice out of the corner of his eye, and Muir had inwardly flinched from the hatred in the other man's face. It wasn't pleasant to feel those waves of loathing accusation coming at you from a total stranger.

At the station, the Inspector had muttered to the desk sergeant: 'Interview room for the big guy— we've got a clever one here. Ring Janice for me and tell her I won't be home.'

'She's going to love you,' the sergeant had commented, and the Inspector had given a grimace.

'Not tonight she's not, unless I can use a can-opener on that bastard.'

Muir had been shown into a small, bare room which contained only a desk and some hard wooden chairs. A man in uniform had followed him in there and taken up a position near the

door. Ten minutes later the Inspector had come in
and sat down opposite Muir and it had begun, but
by then Muir had had time to think the situation
through, and he had decided what he would say.
He was not going to tell the police anything at all
until Cathy had made her own statement. He knew
he hadn't committed a crime, he couldn't be
charged with anything unless someone formally
accused him of one, and once Cathy recovered
consciousness she would tell the police the truth.
Muir wasn't going to jump the gun, he was going
to let Cathy decide what the police were told.

He had looked up at the electric clock ticking on
the wall. Eleven o'clock, he had thought—how
long would it be before Cathy recovered consciousness? How badly injured had she been when
she fell? Sweat had broken out on his forehead as
he remembered the limpness of her body as the
ambulance men lifted her on to the stretcher. The
fall down the stairs had seemed to go on for ever—
Muir had been paralysed, unable to move, rigid
with shock and terror, as he watched her falling. It
had seemed an eternity to him at the time, but it
could only have been a few seconds, yet now every
time he looked up at the clock he mentally saw it
happening again, her body tumbling, crashing
from the wall to the wooden banister and back
again, over and over, while she screamed.

'Mr Ingram, you aren't doing yourself any good
by not answering my questions, you know,' the
Inspector had told him once during the long night.
'Now, let's recap, shall we? You're a reporter with
the *Globe*, you live in Chalk Farm. What are you
doing in Westoak? We've been in touch with your

newspaper and they say you're on leave in France.'

'I'm not in France,' Muir had conceded drily, and the Inspector had looked at him, running a hand over his hair.

'Why are you in Westoak?' The tone had had grim impatience in it.

'I'm staying at the Westoak Grand,' Muir had told him.

'We know where you're staying, Mr Ingram— what we want to know is why? Why did you tell your office you were going to France and why, then, did you come here?'

Muir didn't answer. 'I haven't committed a crime,' he had said again, as he had said fifty times already. 'I have the right to refuse to discuss my private affairs. I want to see my solicitor.'

'Mr Winter tells us that he had never set eyes on you before, nor had he ever heard his daughter mention your name.'

Muir had had no comment to make on that, he hadn't expected that Cathy would mention him to anyone. He looked at the clock again and moved restlessly in his chair. 'How is she? Can you ring the hospital àgain?'

'Worried about her, are you?' the Inspector had asked with a faint sneer. 'Think she may die on you? That would be very unfortunate for you, wouldn't it?'

Muir had turned a white, furious face towards him, his eyes leaping with the fear and grief he was feeling, and for a second he had almost come up out of the chair and gone for the other man. The Inspector had seen the menace in his face, seen his powerful hands flexing, seen the poised rigidity of his body, and he had frozen as he stared at him.

'Yes, you're a nasty piece of work, all right,' he had said, almost to himself. 'Turns you on, does it, knocking them about? She said you hurt her.' He had leaned towards Muir across the desk, his lips writhing with distaste. 'I don't know why you're bothering to drag it out, chum. We've got you nailed on this one—caught dead on the spot, weren't you? You haven't got a hope in hell of getting away with it. Why not do yourself a favour, come clean and let's get it over with.'

Muir had got himself under control again. He had folded his arms and looked at the clock. 'I want to see my solicitor.'

The Inspector had taken a deep breath, Muir had heard him shifting in his chair. It creaked under his weight and he put both hands behind his head, clasping them there while he surveyed Muir in silence.

'When Miss Winter makes a statement . . .' he began, and Muir looked at him sharply.

'Is she still unconscious?' That sounded as though she was still out—was she in a coma? What had she done to herself when she fell? 'Are her injuries serious?' Muir asked huskily.

'The head injury's worrying the hospital,' the Inspector had told him. 'She didn't break any bones, apart from a hairline crack in the skull, but she's pretty badly bruised. She isn't going to die, Mr Ingram—she'll tell us what happened sooner or later, you know. It won't do you any good to keep your mouth shut—as soon as Miss Winter can talk, we'll know what happened.'

Muir had given him a twisted little smile, his

grey eyes ironic. 'Yes,' he had agreed.

It had gone on throughout the night. For a few hours they had left him in a cell to sleep while the Inspector went home, then the Inspector re-appeared and they had resumed the discussion. Eventually, at ten in the morning, Muir's solicitor had shown up and they had had a private talk in the interview room.

Muir had told Sam Walling the truth and Sam had listened, his head bent, so that Muir saw the pink scalp showing through his thinning grey hair. They had known each other for five years—Sam was something of a friend as well as being his solicitor. They often lunched together or had drinks, and Sam was a source of information. Muir often picked his brains about the law or discussed current cases with him.

'You're taking an almighty risk, Muir,' Sam had told him at last, looking up. 'Why don't you let me talk to them, tell them what really happened?'

'I'll wait until Cathy's talked to them.'

'And if she doesn't tell the story you just told me?' Sam had asked drily.

Muir stared at him, his face blank. 'I told you the truth, Sam! You don't think I did it? You don't think I'd rape...'

'Of course I don't,' Sam had said soothingly. 'I know you too well—why on earth should you need to rape any woman? A guy who looks like you? Do me a favour, Muir. Of course I believe you— implicitly. But the police have got tidy minds. What they see is that there's been a nutter lurking about the town, attacking women. The Inspector was very forthcoming, suspiciously so for a policeman, insisted on showing me the reports on this rapist-suspect. Sounded like you, Muir—big guy, tall, dark, wearing a leather jacket and jeans.' He looked at Muir, spreading his hands in a wry little gesture. 'Tailor-made, you see? Then they get a call from this girl's father. Girl's been raped, thrown down a flight of stairs . . .'

'She fell! It was an accident!'

'I believe you—but they won't.'

'Cathy will tell them . . .'

'Will she?' Sam had eyed him with compassion. 'Sorry, Muir, but women are unpredictable witnesses. Emotional, contrary, you never know what they're going to say or do, especially where men are concerned, and I've also seen what she said before she passed out, what she told her father. Said you'd made her do it, you'd hurt her—now, put yourself in the Inspector's place—what would you think when you heard that? She's accused you of rape, Muir, that's what it looks like on the face of it.'

'When she gets over the accident she'll tell them the truth,' Muir insisted. He looked down at the table. 'I love her, Sam.'

Sam was silent. Then he said: 'Question is, old son, does she love you?'

'Yes!' Muir hurled the word at him almost hoarsely, with vehemence.

'Trying to convince me or yourself?'

'Some things you know for certain,' Muir shrugged. 'You don't even need words. Cathy loves me.'

'And this Telford guy?'

'She's fond of him, she feels guilty about him . . .'

'That's bad,' Sam said flatly. 'A guilty woman can be very stupid at times. Guilt makes them do dumb things. If she's very fond of the man and feels guilty about him, she just might lie to protect him.'

Muir had sat staring at him, his brows fixed in a hard frown, and Sam had looked back, watching his face enquiringly.

Muir had shaken his head at last. 'You don't know her, she wouldn't do that to me.'

'I hope not,' Sam had said. 'Because frankly, Muir, you're in quite a tight corner—it's either you or Telford, as I see it. The question is which of you does the lady really care about?' He had got up, tucking his brief case under his arm. 'Well, at least you had the good sense to clam up—it's up to them to decide whether or not they have a good enough case. If they charge you, we'll know your young lady hasn't backed your story up.'

'Could you find out how she is?' Muir had asked, and Sam had nodded and smiled.

'I'll see what I can do—anything else you need? I'll try to get them to release you of course, but I can't hold out much hope that they will.'

'I don't need anything,' Muir had said wearily, and Sam had patted his shoulder with an encouraging smile.

'See you, Muir.'

When he had gone, Muir had sat down again and let his head drop into his hands, his elbows propped on the desk.

Cathy was sitting up in the bed, like a child, her

amber-blonde hair brushed until it gleamed in the morning sunlight. She had slept heavily all night, they had given her a sleeping pill to make sure of that, and this morning she felt grey and empty. She stared at the policeman sitting beside the bed, an expression of something approaching desperation on her face.

'I wish I could remember, I've been trying to, I think until my head aches, but I just can't come up with anything. There's nothing there!'

'Don't upset yourelf, Miss Winter,' Inspector Werrell said in a coaxing, gentle voice, and patted her hand. 'Let's try another tack—does the name Ingram mean anything to you?'

Cathy stared, frowning. 'Ingram? No, should it?'

'You've never heard the name before?'

'I don't think so. Why?'

'Think hard, Miss Winter—do you know anyone by that name?'

Cathy's green eyes widened as she concentrated, biting her lip. 'No, no, I'm sure I don't—what is this all about, Inspector? Why won't you tell me? What happened?' Her voice had risen and was trembling with nerves, her pale face had a fixed intensity in it, as she stared at the policeman.

'Let's just go through it again,' he said. 'You'd been to work, it was a very warm day, you drove straight from the office to Garth House to see your fiancé.'

'I always do visit Stephen every evening,' Cathy explained. 'Always, I see him every day.' There was a haunted uncertainty in her eyes, she lowered them to her hands and the Inspector saw her lips quiver.

'Then you left Garth House and drove back to your own home. Your father was out to dinner with friends. You left Garth House somewhere around eight. Try to think, Miss Winter—do you remember that evening? You drove home and parked the car . . . do you remember that?'

'I don't remember anything,' said Cathy, struggling not to cry. 'Nothing, nothing—there's nothing there.'

The Inspector got up as the Ward Sister shot into the room, indignation in her face. 'I know, I'm going, Sister, I'm going.' He looked at Cathy, who had put her head back against the pillows, trembling. 'If you remember anything, Miss Winter, anything at all, you just tell Sister you want to see me and I'll be round to see you the minute I get the call.'

Cathy nodded without speaking, and he went out. She stared at the pink roses in blank silence— why couldn't she remember?

Muir stood in the line of other men, feeling the sunlight on his face and waiting with a fixed tension for the girl to walk past. He had been warned not to move his head, not to look at her, but they had not told him who she was. He swallowed, his throat rough. Was it Cathy? He didn't know how he was going to control himself if it was—at the moment he was trembling, his teeth tight. The police wouldn't be having an identity parade if Cathy had told them the truth. What had she told them?

He heard the girl moving, the rustle of her skirt, then she paused in front of him, staring. Muir's

eyes flickered, he couldn't help the quick glance,
he had to know if it was Cathy.

It wasn't. The face was that of a stranger, a
young woman with smooth dark hair. She walked
away slowly and a moment later he heard her
behind him, then he felt her hand brush his
shoulder. Muir's brows drew together. What was
going on? Who was she?

'Come on, Mr Ingram,' he was told, and hustled
back to the interview room. A moment later Sam
came in and put his briefcase down on the table,
staring grimly at Muir, who stared back, trying to
read his friend's expression.

'What was all that about? What's going on?'

'They've given me five minutes with you,' Sam
said gruffly. 'Then they're going to charge you
with attempted rape.'

Muir stiffened in his chair. 'You can't be
serious!'

'I told you you were running an almighty risk,'
Sam said. 'Women are unpredictable.'

'Cathy told them I'd raped her?' Muir couldn't
believe it was happening to him; his face lost every
shred of colour, he felt as if he'd been kicked in the
stomach by a mule. 'I don't believe it, she wouldn't
do that to me.'

'She's far too cute for that,' Sam agreed with
distate. 'She's claiming to have amnesia.'

'What?'

'Can't remember what happened,' said Sam,
sneering. 'Can't remember your name, doesn't
know you, never heard of you in her life.'

Muir's face locked into a rigid rictus of pain,
and Sam turned and walked away, an expression

of pity in his eyes. With his back to Muir he said slowly: 'I warned you, Muir—you can't trust women. She's turned you in. It was either you or this Telford character, so the little lady decided it was going to be you who got the knife in his back.'

Muir's throat moved convulsively as he swallowed, he was white under his tan and his eyes had a harsh, fixed expression. There was a long silence, then he said: 'But if she claims she doesn't remember anything, how can they charge me with rape? It would have to be Cathy who pressed charges, surely? She would have to give evidence at the trial, and how could she do that if she doesn't remember what ha ened?'

'That's why the police delayed so long, they were trying to think of a way of holding you until Cathy could give evidence. A couple of nights before you went to Cathy's home, a man broke into the nurses' home in town and tried to rape one of the nurses. This guy fitted your description, Muir.'

'You told me,' Muir said shortly, his voice flat.

'You were identified by the girl who was attacked.' Sam told him, turning to watch him.

'Oh, God,' Muir muttered, dropping his face into his hands.

'They need to charge you if they're going to hold you indefinitely and they didn't want to let you go.' Sam came round the table and roughly patted his shoulder. 'I'm sorry, Muir, we haven't got much time. I want you to listen to me very carefully. We're going to have to give them your side of it now. Once you've been charged it could be very nasty for you. They have a pretty solid weight of circumstantial evidence against you, and the fact that you won't talk is damning. I understand why you've held back until now— you've been trying to protect her. But it's either you or her, don't you see that? You must let me tell them the truth.'

Muir nodded, letting his hands fall to the table. His face was harsh and bitterly angry. 'You're right. Okay, tell them everything.'

'Right,' said Sam. 'Any other reporters at this conference? Anyone who knows you?'

Muir frowned, perspiration on his forehead. 'Graham Birkett from the *Holiday Trade Gazette*,' he said slowly. 'A couple of others came down from Paris, French fellows, I don't remember their names—Graham might know.'

'They saw you with Cathy Winter? They'd remember the two of you?'

'I don't know, maybe—I suppose so, we were together all the time.' Muir's jaw was rigid. 'All the time,' he muttered, a muscle ticking beside his mouth. 'The bitch, the lying little bitch!'

Sam stared at the angry scratches along his cheek and neck. 'I've got to ask you, this, Muir— was there a struggle between you and Cathy?'

'I didn't rape her!' Muir exploded, lifting his head and glaring at him. 'I didn't rape her!'

'I wasn't supposing you had,' Sam said soothingly. 'But was there a fight? How did you get those scratches?'

'We quarrelled,' Muir admitted, and an angry light came into his eyes. 'The police saw them, don't think they missed them. The doctor took a good look at them when I had a medical examination.' He turned his head and gave Sam a long, bitter stare. 'They took the clothes I was wearing, you know. Everything—they stripped me to the skin and I had to sit here in a blanket until they brought some of my clothes from the hotel.'

'Standard procedure,' Sam shrugged with a faint sigh. 'You won't be denying that you had sex with Cathy Winter, anyway.'

'No,' said Muir with force, his voice harsh, 'I won't.'

Sam turned towards the door. 'I'll tell the Inspector you're ready to make a full statement—tell him everything, Muir, be as frank with him as you were with me.'

Muir nodded, his face tense, then he broke out: 'She's lying, Sam, I know she is—she's pretending she doesn't remember—it's far too convenient, I don't believe she has forgotten. The little—I'd like to kill her!'

'Calm down, for heaven's sake,' Sam said urgently, shooting a look at the closed door. 'Don't talk like that in front of the police.' His eyes were anxious as he watched Muir's grim, angry face, saw the violence seething in the grey eyes. 'Muir you're in trouble, bad trouble. You've got to keep your head, don't lose your cool now. She isn't worth it.'

'No,' Muir agreed, his lips straight and hard. 'She isn't worth it.'

Sam went out and left him sitting at the table, staring into space. When the Inspector came into the room Muir looked at him, his face calm now. In a level voice he made his statement and the

Inspector listened while a constable took down what Muir was saying.

'So you followed Miss Winter back to Westoak,' said the Inspector a few moments later. 'You and she quarrelled, on your own admission, on the last night of this conference—she told you she was engaged and made it clear she did not want to continue to see you, yet you followed her here.'

Muir's face took on a dark red flush, his jaw tightened. He nodded without speaking.

'You were violently angry when you heard she was engaged to another man?'

Muir looked at him, on the point of erupting into bitter fury, then thought better of it and was silent.

'You've been identified as the man who broke into the nurses' home, Mr Ingram, and I'm going to charge you with that—as soon as Miss Winter is well enough to talk we'll see how far her version of what happened matches yours.'

Muir sat there, his hands clenched on the table, his face tightly under control, but his mind was chaotic and he thought of Cathy with an intensity of contempt and hatred which made his body tremble so much that when the Inspector asked him to stand up so that he could be formally charged, Muir almost knocked over his chair, his movement jerky and stiff.

He saw Sam again shortly afterwards. 'Our priority is to find witnesses to prove you were in London the night the nurses' home was broken into—is there anything I can do for you?' Sam asked.

'Nothing,' said Muir. 'The only thing I want is to get my hands round Cathy Winter's throat.'

'Don't be a damned fool,' urged Sam, gripping his arm. 'Now listen to me—they have to bring you up in front of the magistrates tomorrow morning, and when they do I'll apply for bail and get you out of here, but they're bound to make it a condition that you leave Westoak at once and only return when you're wanted for the first hearing. At all costs, make no threats against Cathy Winter. You mustn't try to see her or get in touch with her. If you do, it will go against you.'

Muir frowned. 'You think they'll let me out?'

'I think there's a good chance. You're of good character, you've never been in trouble before and the case against you is far from being watertight. The police will oppose bail, but I think I'll manage to talk the magistrates into it.'

'I can put up bail myself,' said Muir, and Sam shook his head.

'Your editor's already offered.' He grinned at Muir. 'Greater trust hath no newspaper—he's so sure you're innocent he said they'd put up whatever was wanted. Of course, he's expecting some redhot exclusives out of it after you've been proved innocent; inside stories about police treatment of a rape suspect, that sort of thing.'

'Tell him he can go to hell,' snapped Muir, and Sam laughed.

'That's my boy!' Walking to the door he looked back, smiled. 'You'll be free tomorrow, Muir, and I'll drive you back to London myself—and you'll stay there.'

Twenty-four hours later, Muir sat in the front passenger seat of Sam's car, staring ahead at the unwinding road. He had the windows rolled right down and the cool, fresh clean air blowing through his black hair, over his grateful skin. After the hours spent in the police station he found the light of the open sky almost blinding, but although he was so relieved to have been released his mind was bitterly occupied by thoughts of Cathy, and his face was grim.

CHAPTER FIVE

CATHY came out of the front door of the cottage and paused to inhale the drenching fragrance of the roses, her eyes lazily following a tiny copper-coloured butterfly as it flew past. It was a fine August morning; the sky blue, the air clear and hot, the hills veiled in a shimmering heat haze.

She had been home for almost a week. She had not recovered her memory, the lost month remained lost, although she had spent a number of hours with the hospital psychiatrist, having tests on the electro-encephalograph machine, lying back like someone in a space age hairdresser's, while her brain waves were monitored on unrolling streams of white paper. The process had been very tedious and time-consuming, involving lengthy preparations while the electrodes were carefully fixed to her scalp. Her hair had been sticky with the glue they had used; it had been a terrible job getting rid of it afterwards. The result had revealed nothing except that so far as could be seen she had suffered no brain damage.

'Then why can't I remember?' she had asked the psychiatrist, who had picked up a pencil and made bizarre doodles on his blotting paper as he spoke, his brow creased.

'The simple answer to that is that you don't want to remember.'

'Why don't I?'

'I couldn't tell you,' he said without looking up.
'You will have to tell me.'

'But I can't when I don't know what it is I've
forgotten,' Cathy protested with a flicker of
impatience and he smiled to himself, annoying her
even more. He was a man whose most usual
expression was one of superiority. 'Why won't
anyone tell me what happened? What sort of
accident did I have?'

'We want you to remember naturally,' he
explained. 'The mind is a very curious machine—if
we told you what we thought had happened, your
mind might start to construct a story that fitted
what you've been told, and then we might never
find out what really happened. We have to wait
for you to bring the truth out of wherever you've
hidden it.' He looked up, smiling blandly, and
Cathy eyed him with dislike. She got the feeling
that he saw her as some sort of laboratory white
mouse on whose brain he was conducting an
experiment. Cathy did not like being an experiment.

'When can I go home?' she asked, and he
surprised her by saying: 'Tomorrow. You're more
or less fit now. Stay off work, of course, and rest
as much as you can. I'll see you in Outpatients in a
week's time.'

Next day her father had arrived at the hospital
with a suitcase full of clothes and she had dressed
and driven home with him. They had talked like
strangers, but then how else had they ever talked?
Her father had always been distant from her, she
had always known she had failed him, she was not
the child he wanted. For as long as she could

remember, Cathy had felt guilty because she couldn't live up to the standard her father set for her. When she was younger she had often felt, like Alice in Looking-Glass Land, that she had to run very fast to stay in the same place. Living up to her father had been very tiring. A sense of guilty failure was very depressing to carry around with you all the time. Cathy had grown up with a strong desire to please him, to please everyone around her, to do what was expected of her, and the older she got the more complicated life became.

The only person who seemed relaxed with her was Jennie. She had visited the hospital a number of times, bringing news of the office, little bits of gossip to make Cathy laugh. Jennie had a way of putting things which was wickedly funny, it could make her victims cringe if they heard her.

'It costs an arm and a leg to so much as speak to Carol now,' she said. 'We're thinking of having the main entrance widened or she won't be able to get her head through it soon!'

Cathy had given her a grin. 'Mrs Telford told me she was doing some of my work—enjoying herself, is she?'

'On cloud nine,' Jennie agreed. 'She sent her love to you, by the way—she said she hoped you'd be back at work soon, may God forgive her.'

Cathy was always sorry when Jennie left, she felt almost normal, listening to her, and when she got home she had been delighted to have Jennie dropping in for an hour or two each evening after work.

Stephen came to see her, too, of course, but

Cathy always felt so strung-up during his visits. She wanted to see him, yet she was afraid of him, afraid of the tension his arrival always brought her—not that Stephen ever said anything or did anything which could explain why the sight of him made her spirits sink and her nerves begin to burn with a nervous fire. When he had gone, she felt exhausted, every nerve-end burnt out.

Seeing him made her want to cry, but why should it? Sometimes she thought she was going out of her mind, imagining the uneasiness she felt all around her, and it was her own uncertainty about it which was so distressing. She could not bear the sheer misery of not knowing what was wrong. If only someone would say something, tell her what had happened—didn't they see that she was going round the bend?

Even Mrs Telford, usually so tough and decisive, seemed different when she saw her. Every time she brought Stephen, she spent a few minutes talking to Cathy; usually about the firm, giving her the latest news of what was going on at the office, but, although she was brisk and matter-of-fact, when she went she always left Cathy with the same impression everyone gave her—a strong sense of uneasiness, which was not Cathy's imagination, she was sure of it. She saw it flickering in their eyes, heard it in their voices.

When she looked at herself in her little compact mirror when she was alone, she half expected her face to show some difference, but apart from being pale and having some fading bruises on her skin, she looked the same. Even her green eyes showed no visible trace of the emptiness behind them.

Cathy got no clues from her reflection.

Her car was parked outside on the grass verge, she unlocked it and got into the driving seat, feeling slightly nervous. She hadn't driven since she got home, but there had to be a first time and she was quite fit now; no longer having headaches, her body no longer aching with bruises. Starting the car, she began to drive down the road. It was a narrow lane with high hedges on either side, the scent of privet thick on the air. As Cathy came towards a blind corner another car rocketed round it, swerving violently at the sight of her car. Cathy automatically pulled in closer to the edge of the road and heard behind her the screech of tyres, and glancing into her wing mirror she saw, to her amazement, the other car turning in the road. Cathy accelerated once she had turned the corner, hearing the other car zooming up behind her. The driver put his hand on his horn and kept it there, the angry blare of the sound making her jump.

What on earth did he think he was doing, hooting at her like that? It had hardly been her fault if he had nearly driven into the hedge, he had been the one driving like a lunatic, and he was driving like one now. Surely he didn't imagine he could pass her on a lane as narrow as this? Cathy watched him in the mirror, frowning. She couldn't see the driver's face; the sun dazzled across his windscreen turning it into a sheet of gold, but she was sure she had never seen the car before. She knew most of the local cars, and, judging by the way he was driving, this was not a local man; he drove like a city-dweller, impatient and in a hurry to get somewhere. If he wanted to pass her, he would take his life in his own hands. Cathy wasn't scraping along the hedge to give him any more room. The way this lane twisted and turned, overtaking was a dangerous game, he was liable to end up smashing into someone else, as he almost had into her.

She turned slowly into the road leading to Garth House, expecting the car behind her to take the road that went back into Westoak, but it followed her, still hooting. She automatically checked the instruments to see if she had left a sidelight on, or if anything was wrong with the car, but just as she reached the gate of Stephen's house she saw the other car start to come out to overtake her.

Cathy spun the wheel and shot up the drive towards Garth House, fuming. That man had been a maniac—What had he been playing at?

She braked and only then realised that the other car was right behind her. Before Cathy had opened her door to get out, the driver of the car behind was out of his seat and racing towards her. A second later, her door was yanked open and she found herself looking up into menacing grey eyes.

'What . . .' Cathy had begun before she looked up, and then she felt a blinding shock hit her, her words died on her stiff, frozen lips and she sat there motionless, staring, while all the colour left her face and she heard in her head an anguished sound without words, a bitter silent protest as the wall protecting her from memories she could not face crumbled and fell for ever.

He leant on the top of the car, his black head bent to stare at her, and watched her with icy intensity.

'What's the matter, Cathy? Can't you act quite so convincingly when I'm your audience? Surely you could make an attempt? Give me one of your wide-eyed, pleading little smiles, ask me who I am, what I'm doing here. After all, you never saw me before in your life, did you? You've never even heard my name, I mean nothing to you!'

The savagery in his tone shrivelled her, she put out a shaking hand. 'Muir, don't . . .' She hadn't fitted it all together yet, she was lost in a confused haze of jumbled memories, knowing only that Muir was violently angry with her, that he was looking at her with hatred and contempt which made her feel sick.

He ignored her hand. 'Get out of there,' he ordered curtly, stepping back, and Cathy shakily obeyed, stumbling as she stood upright beside him. Muir slammed her car door and stood there, his hands on his lean hips, looking her up and down with a twisted smile.

'You weren't expecting to see me, of course. Thought I was safely miles away in London, did you? Did that ice-cold little brain of yours work out that so long as they believed you'd lost your memory they'd keep me away from you? Well, they did, of course—I was warned that they'd throw the book at me if I came within a mile of you, and I'm not fool enough to risk any more trouble, so I stayed away. But you had a stroke of bad luck last night, darling, or should I say your good luck ran out?'

'What are you talking about?' Cathy asked, flinching at his biting tone, that hostile stare. Inside her head, she was fitting it all together now;

the scattered jigsaw puzzle of that vanished month, realising with a pang of shame why she had wanted to forget, why Muir was so angry with her. She had denied him; deliberately cut him out of her memory, and it would do her no good to tell him that she had not done so knowingly, Muir wouldn't forgive her for it.

'I thought the police might have been in touch, but maybe they'll be getting around to you later today. They rang me early this morning and asked me to come to Westoak as soon as I could.' His eyes focused on her, their dark pupils hard and glittering. 'They arrested someone else last night, breaking into the nurses' home. He's been identified, but, more important, he confessed to having tried before. The charge against me has been dropped.'

'Charge against you?' Cathy repeated falteringly, and got a coldly savage smile.

'Cut the phoney bewilderment, I don't buy it— you'll never pull the wool over my eyes again, darling, you can be sure of that.'

'I don't know what you're talking about,' she protested, backing until she felt the sunwarmed metal of the car bonnet behind her. Muir took a long stride to come closer, his mouth a bitter line in his bronzed face.

'I've spent a lot of time working out precisely what I'd like to do to you, Cathy—don't push your luck too far or I might put one of my plans into operation, and strangle you slowly with my bare hands.'

She didn't dare to move, her throat was raw with fear and guilt. He stared into her green eyes, his face only inches away, and she saw a muscle jerking in his cheek.

'I'd like to kill you,' he said hoarsely, and she believed him, she froze like a small animal in a trap listening to the tread of the hunter, tremors of terror passing through her.

'I know you're angry with me——' she began, and he laughed, but the sound was more like a snarl.

'Lady, is that an understatement!'

'I didn't want to lose my memory,' she protested, but that cold little voice in her head asked: didn't you? and a second later, like a savage echo, Muir asked the same question.

'Didn't you? Oh, but I think you did—that was the plan, wasn't it? How soon did you work it out? It was clever, too, I'll grant you that. You've got brains, darling. I won't underestimate you again, you can be sure of that. I'll watch you like a hawk!'

He was watching her like one now; his face brooding, menacing, his lean body vibrating with the desire to hurt her, his hands flexing involuntarily at his sides, the long fingers curling like predatory talons.

'I'm telling the truth . . .' Cathy began, close to tears, and he laughed again, even more harshly.

'I wonder the word doesn't stick in your lying little throat!'

Cathy flinched, so terrified of the darkness in his face that she stammered: 'You . . . you haven't explained about the charge you said the police had dropped—what charge? What were you being charged with? They didn't suspect you . . .'

'You damned well know they did!' he erupted. 'It was you who put it into their heads in the first place!'

'Me?' Cathy thought she was hearing things, she stared, eyes enormous in her white face. 'But . . .'

'When did you decide to do it, Cathy? When you realised your father had arrived? Did a spot of very rapid calculation, did you, and decide to accuse me of rape?'

'Rape?' The word came out loudly, her voice rising, and some wood pigeons took alarm and flapped up into the blue sky, with a clatter which Cathy heard without looking round.

'Not bad, you almost convince me,' Muir grated icily. 'You're good, darling, you're superb, butter wouldn't melt in your mouth.' He paused, then imitated her scathingly: 'Rape?' He dropped her tone and said: 'If you don't switch off the performance, Cathy, I'll do you an injury, so help me God. I don't want any more of your lies.'

Her eyes burned with unshed tears. 'I haven't been lying!' Haven't you? her own mind asked her. Did you really forget him? Or were you refusing to remember because you just could not face up to the situation? How much of her loss of memory had been genuine, and how much had she somehow managed to hide every trace of Muir from her own mind by some sort of mental sleight of hand? The minute she saw him she had remembered him, she couldn't deny that.

'The minute you saw me you magically remembered,' Muir sneered, and she looked at him in dazed surprise, wondering if it was sheer coincidence that he had repeated her own thoughts for the second time, or if he was picking them up by telepathy. Or was it simply that they were both thinking along the same lines and arriving at the same conclusions but from a very different jumping off point? Muir believed she had knowingly lied, and Cathy saw he would never believe her protests.

'I still don't understand why the police charged you with anything,' she whispered. 'Muir, honestly, I didn't accuse you—how could I? I don't remember.'

'That was what was so cute,' said Muir. 'You pointed an accusing finger at me then conveniently lost your memory so that you didn't actually have to swear anything on oath. But the police didn't need you—they had another eye-witness, didn't they? This girl from the nurses' home! So they wheeled me in front of her and she picked me out and I was charged with that.' He leaned towards her, putting his hands on the car bonnet to support his weight, and Cathy shrank as she felt his thighs touch hers; the powerful male body arched above her in a silent threat enforced by the rage in his eyes. 'I had to get my editor to bail me out,' Muir went on. 'The story's half round London, my friends can't meet my eyes. When I walk into a pub people whisper and look at me out of the corners of their eyes. I feel as though I've been branded, and all because of you, you . . .'

'Don't! she whispered before he said the words.

'Don't what? Don't describe you too accurately? Can't you take it, Cathy? Don't you want to know what you are? How have you managed to look into mirrors all this time?'

Her spine hurt, she was spreadeagled under him, almost lying on the car, their bodies so close that she could hear his heart beating under the white shirt he wore, she could see the smallest pore in his skin, pick up the lingering trace of his aftershave. Her green eyes slid sideways to escape the bitter stare pinning her like a moth on a card, she trembled and felt Muir watch her, the violence inside him only just controlled, his eyes dangerous.

'I didn't know about the police,' she said pleadingly. 'Nobody would tell me anything, I had no idea any of this was happening.'

'Oh, of course not!' His mouth twisted viciously. 'Forget the speech, Cathy. Let's get one thing straight—from now on, you're telling the truth, the whole truth and nothing but the truth, and you're starting right away with the police. You're coming into Westoak with me now and you're going to tell them I didn't rape you, you're going to tell them you fell down that staircase by accident, you're going to tell them that the only thing I'm guilty of is making a bloody fool of myself about a cheating little bitch who doesn't think twice about pulling a doublecross that makes Judas look like Snow White!'

His anger made her wince, but she asked nervously: 'I don't understand why they think you raped me. Muir, honestly, I didn't accuse you of doing anything of the sort!'

'I was there, remember? When you fell down the stairs? You said to your father: he made me, he hurt me—I heard you, Cathy, so don't lie!'

'Oh,' she said, on a painful indrawn breath, remembering, and Muir's eyes watched her face, reading the admission she couldn't suppress.

'I was a stranger in the town, they were hunting for a man who fitted my description—I didn't have a prayer, did I? You set me up.'

'No,' she denied, 'you can't believe that, you know I wouldn't do such a thing.'

'What do I know about you? You're a liar and a coward, and above all you're a woman. I should have remembered that you can't trust a woman further than you can see her.' He straightened and looked her up and down with distaste. 'And now you're coming along with me to see the police, and this time you'll tell them what really happened!'

'I must speak to Stephen first,' she said unhappily. 'I can't let him hear it from anyone else, he'll be so hurt.'

Muir's mouth twisted bitterly. 'And we can't have that, can we? He's a very rich man. What fairy story will you spin him, Cathy? How are you going to wriggle your way out of it? No, don't tell me, I don't want to know.' He swung on his heel to walk away, saying: 'Just don't take too long breaking it to him—and don't lose your memory again, because it won't work this time. I'll choke the truth out of you if I have to!'

She turned shakily towards the house and halted in her tracks as she saw Stephen standing there, leaning on his stick. Cathy's widening eyes searched his pale face and saw the pain his eyes did not disguise from her. How much of what she and Muir had been saying had he overheard? Enough to guess at the truth, that much she realised—his face was drawn and shadowed, and she hated herself as she looked at him.

Muir was just getting into his car, she heard the door open and slam, then the grate of his quick steps as he came back towards them, having seen Stephen in the doorway.

Stephen didn't even look in his direction. He held out a hand to Cathy, his mouth unsteady, and although there was sadness in those hazel eyes there was no violence, no hatred; the bitter, searing emotion which Muir had flung at her just now was not reflected in Stephen's face.

She took a step, trembling, then another, then Stephen's arm closed round her and pressed her face into his shoulder, his hand stroking her hair.

Cathy let the tired tears come; she had been holding them back while she was facing Muir, but Stephen's gentle gesture snapped the last thread of her control and she wept helplessly.

Muir's engine started with a roar, she heard the tyres screech as he backed and accelerated with a violent swerve out of the gates.

'We'd better go into the house,' Stephen said above her head. 'Don't cry, Cathy—don't. I hate to hear you cry like that.'

'I'm sorry, Stephen, I'm so sorry.' There was so much she had to say to him, but that was what it all came to in the end—she was sorry, she felt so guilty she wished she was dead, she hated herself far more than Muir hated her.

'I've made such a mess of everything,' she whispered.

'Can we go inside?' Stephen asked, and then she felt the shake in his body and with a new pang of guilt realised how tiring it was for him to stand like this with her leaning on him.

'I'm sorry,' she said again, lifting her head and putting an arm around his waist in a quick movement.

They walked back into the house and Cathy saw Nandy standing in the high-ceilinged hall, watching them with a stiff, blank face. Cathy could not face her, she looked away—had Nandy heard, too? Did Nandy realise what had really happened?

This was why she had erased all memory of Muir, this was the core of her pain and uncertainty, her fear and shame—her whole world had been built up around Stephen, his family, their life in Westoak, the future they were going to share together, and when she met Muir that future was shattered into tiny pieces. All the people she knew, liked, cared about, loved, had been part of that future—when she fell in love with Muir she was presented with an impossible choice between him and everything she had ever known, her whole life. Nandy and Jennie and Mrs Telford, her father and Stephen—they would all be divided from her from now on, they would no longer be part of her life.

That was what she hadn't been able to face. It hadn't been Stephen alone she had been protecting—she had been struggling desperately to save the familiar, reassuring certainties with which she had lived until now.

What, after all, did she know about Muir? They had come very close very quickly in the week they spent together at Nice, but she had hidden so much from him—how much had he hidden from her? People are so multi-faceted, so complex; they can choose which side of themselves they present to strangers, they can deceive and mislead without being aware what they are doing. Under the spell of sexual excitement; their senses heightened, their wits sharpened, people move out of their normal character, charged with a brilliance which cannot last, which is unreal and will fade in time. Love makes liars of us all, Cathy thought, we're like those birds whose plumage is brightest when they are looking for a mate. Everyday life can never match that brief radiance.

Muir was the dark stranger, the intruder, and she hadn't been able to face the conflict he set up inside her, the choice between everything she had ever known and the sudden, intense desire she had felt for him. Her common sense had warned her that if Stephen had not been so ill for so long, she might never have felt a thing for Muir. How much of what she did feel was due to a frustrated drive for fulfilment? If she had been sleeping with Stephen, if they had been married two years ago, she would have been too happy to look at another man.

Stephen painfully lowered himself into a chair. 'Sit down, Cathy.'

She sat on a footstall next to him without stopping to think—it was where she always sat, close to him, her head on a level with his knees.

'Tell me about him,' Stephen said in a calm voice. 'Begin at the beginning—when did you meet him, and how?'

She told him without looking at him and left out nothing, but she did not dare to look at Stephen, she kept her eyes fixed on her hands. When her low, husky voice stopped, he sighed.

'Poor fellow!'

Cathy looked up, then, taken aback, not expecting him to show Muir sympathy, and Stephen made a face at her. 'Putting myself in his place, it must have been a real kick in the teeth to be accused of rape, epecially when he thought it was you who'd accused him.'

'But I didn't!'

'Not knowingly, perhaps, but he wasn't to know that. I can see why he's in a pretty aggressive mood at the moment, though. Your amnesia must have seemed far too convenient.'

'Stephen, I did forget, I did! You've got to believe me!'

He looked down at her, his hazel eyes gentle, the sun shining through the window behind him and picking out stray golden lights in his dull brown hair. 'I've known you for too many years to doubt your word, Cathy. People don't change that much. You never could lie deliberately, and you've always been one to worry about every little thing. Of course I believe you. You didn't want to remember, but I don't suspect you forgot deliberately, you were protecting yourself. You just shut off all that part of your memory until you felt you could cope with it—and now that you're physically fit again you've had to remember.'

'The minute I saw him,' she whispered, and Stephen's hands clenched on the arms of the chair. Cathy looked up at him quickly, but his face was calm.

'In one way I'm relieved,' he said, almost to himself.

Taken aback, Cathy echoed: 'Relieved?' Her voice was incredulous.

'When my mother told me you'd been attacked and raped I almost went crazy. I felt so helpless, I couldn't do anything. The thought of you . . .' He broke off, sighing unevenly. 'At least you didn't have to go through that. My God, Cathy, I spent a sleepless night trying not to imagine what had been done to you!'

Cathy leaned her head on his knees, stifling a sob, and he touched her hair briefly. They sat in silence for a long moment, then Stephen very gently pushed her head away, and Cathy shivered and sat upright.

'You're in love with him, aren't you? You say you aren't sure, but I think you are, darling,' said Stephen, and Cathy couldn't meet his eyes, biting her lips.

'I wish you'd told me,' he said, and the fact that there was no real reproach in his voice, only sadness, made it much worse.

'Stephen, I'm so sorry.'

'It isn't your fault—I half expected it . . .'

'Expected it?' She looked up, and he gave her a wry pretence of a smile.

'Of course—you're young and very pretty, you have a right to some fun while you're still young, you need sex as much as any other woman does—I couldn't give you either. Why do you think I wouldn't marry you? What sort of marriage could we have had? I wasn't marrying you until I could make love to you the way I want to . . .'

Cathy winced and he looked away, his face tight. 'We've had enough lies, Cathy—I'm not going to add to them by pretending I don't want you and love you exactly the way I always have.'

Her head drooped, her hands clenched in her lap, twisting miserably. Stephen sighed after a silent moment.

'You'd better go down to Westoak and tell the police the truth, now, Cathy. Best get it over with—we can talk later.'

She got to her feet shakily and looked at him with uncertainty and bitter regret. 'Stephen . . .' What if her fears came true? What if Stephen gave up because she had walked out on him like this?

He looked up and gave her another wry mock smile, his mouth uneven 'And don't look so tragic—I'll live with it, I've learned to live with worse than this and discovered to my surprise that I've a lot more strength than I ever thought I had. We never know what we can bear until we have to bear it, Cathy.'

'I hate myself,' she muttered. 'I wish you'd shout at me, Stephen, tell me what you think of me, don't be so kind, you make me feel terrible.'

A flash of dry humour crossed his thin face. 'I'm afraid that is what *you'll* have to bear, Cathy. It's the only punishment I'll ever inflict on you. I can't hate you just because you're human, even to please you.'

She wanted to kiss him, but she knew he would shrink away if she did, so she kissed her fingers and placed them on his forehead; then she went out of the room, past Nandy's wooden figure, out of the house into the brilliant, ironic sunlight, which mocked her as she drove away, her eyes dazzled by it, and by the hot tears forcing themselves out of her as she drove.

She spent the next hour at the police station talking to the Inspector. He kept his eyes on the desk most of the time, nodding now and then, but to her relief he showed no sign either of shock or contempt. Occasionally she thought there was curiosity in his face, but then it vanished again as she answered his polite questions.

Cathy had been terrified of seeing Muir again, but when she left there was no sign of him. His car was parked in a corner of the police car park, however, so she knew he was still around. She did not go back to Garth House, she drove home and packed a suitcase rapidly, her hands trembling in her haste. She had to get away before Muir caught up with her. When she had put the case into the boot of her car she wrote a note to her father telling him a bald outline of the truth and adding that she had decided to go away for a while to think things over. She put the note where he would see it, on the table, and left the cottage. She had not told her father where she intended to go—he might tell Muir, and Cathy could not face Muir again. Her only thought was escape from the tangled chaos she had made of her whole life.

She didn't even reach her car. As she opened the garden gate, Muir's car swerved to a halt on the lane and he leapt out, cold mockery in his eyes as he saw Cathy's panic-stricken face.

'Going somewhere?' he drawled, then his hand shot out and grabbed her arm before she could run. 'Oh, no, you don't, lady, you aren't going anywhere!'

CHAPTER SIX

CATHY took a deep breath, looking up at him out of frightened, cat-green eyes, her mind hunting for a way of escaping from him. She had her back to the wall, she was entirely on her own with him, with no one to help her, and after a moment of frozen panic she felt the adrenalin of fear pumping through her veins. She lifted her head, her chin defiant, and faced him because she had no other choice.

'I'm on my way to see someone and I haven't got time to talk. I've been to the police, I told them the truth, there's nothing else for us to say to each other.'

'Wrong,' Muir said tersely. 'I have a great deal to say to you, and I don't give a twopenny curse where you're going.' He strode through the gate, dragging her after him, tethered helplesly by that merciless hand, but holding back, struggling and pulling away at every step like a reluctant child. When they got to the front door of the cottage, Muir thrust out his free hand.

'Key.'

Cathy stubbornly looked the other way, the wind blowing her blonde hair into a confused mass of unruly curls.

'You heard me,' Muir muttered through barely parted lips, then his fingers curled round her chin and wrenched her head back towards him. 'Don't annoy me, Cathy. I'm in just the mood to lose my temper, don't push me too far. Give me your key, and make it snappy!'

She dared one glance at his set face, then she fumbled in her pocket and brought out the key. Muir took it and opened the door, walked through it into the cottage pulling her after him. In the sitting-room he almost threw her into a chair and stood beside her, glaring at her with furious grey eyes.

'I ought to hit you, and I'm still considering it, so do yourself a favour, don't budge a muscle from that chair or you'll regret it!'

She shrank back, clutching the arms of the chair, shivering as though with icy cold. Muir glanced around the room, while she watched nervously. His tanned skin was drawn tightly over his cheekbones, giving a dangerous cast to his features which warned her that he meant the threat he had just made.

'Where's your father?' he demanded.

'At the school.'

'I though it was closed for the summer.'

'He has a lot of paperwork to catch up on.'

Muir nodded, then said: 'Has he got any whisky?'

'Whisky?' Cathy repeated blankly, and he looked back at her, his eyes skimming over her in a slow appraisal which made her stiffen in new alarm.

'I need a drink,' he said, his mouth twisting, and somehow the curt confession made Cathy feel better; it made him more human, less steely.

'In the cabinet over there,' she said, beginning to get up. 'Shall I . . .'

'Stay where you are!' Muir commanded, and she prickled with resentment at the sharp tone. 'I'll get it myself.'

She watched him walk over and open the cabinet, get out a glass and a bottle of whisky. He poured himself a good finger of the drink, added some soda and then turned to survey her with the glass in his hand, leaning against the top of the cabinet in a lounging attitude. Cathy's eyes hurriedly moved away from him.

'What did Telford have to say?' he demanded, and she decided not to answer the harsh question. He had no right to know and she had no intention of telling him. Although she was not looking towards him she felt his eyes fixed on her, probing the averted curve of her profile, and her skin prickled with awareness.

'Forgiving, was he?' Muir asked in icy derision. 'What exactly did you tell him, Cathy? That sleeping with me had been a mistake? That you were sorry the minute it happened? Did you tell him you wished it had never happened, that it was him you really loved?' He paused, watching her, and Cathy ignored him. 'Answer me, damn you!' he muttered harshly.

'Why should I?' Cathy turned her head then and met his stare head-on without flinching. 'What happened between me and Stephen has nothing to do with you . . .'

'Oh, you're wrong,' retorted Muir, slamming his glass down with a violence that made her jump. 'It's very much my business.' He took a step towards her, his lean body tensely held, then stopped, staring towards the table. Cathy looked

in that direction, too, puzzled by his expression for
a moment. When she realised what he was staring
at, it was too late for her to do anything. He had
taken two strides and was picking up the letter she
had left for her father.

'What's this?' he asked.

'Put it down, it isn't addressed to you!'

'I can see who it's addressed to—why are you
leaving notes for your father?'

'Mind your own business!'

Muir looked down at the envelope and then tore
it open. Cathy came out of the chair, trembling
with anger. 'Don't you read that letter! You have
no right!'

His hand held her off as she tried to snatch it
from him. His hard gaze skated down the shakily
written lines and Cathy's face burned as she
watched him reading her unhappy explanation to
her father.

His face gave her no clues as to his reaction; she
watched the thick dark lashes flicking against his
skin, his mouth straight and unyielding, and
wished she knew him better. Instant, intense
attraction was no basis for any sort of understanding—she had no idea of how Muir's mind worked,
she only knew that he was a man capable of
dangerous impulses and fierce emotions. He might
angrily deny that he had raped her, but in a sense
he had taken her by force, and he knew it: he had
done it quite deliberately, it had been a calculated
gamble. Cathy found that thought alarming. Muir
would use force if he had to—that was the only
certain fact she knew about him, and that
disturbed her.

He looked up and the grey eyes held a glittering threat. 'So you were running, were you?' The tone mocked icily, then the ice melted and there was rage in his voice. 'You little coward, is that your only answer to things you can't handle? You always run away, do you?'

She flinched from the contempt, but screwed up her courage to answer. 'I needed time to think, is that so surprising?'

'You were bolting,' Muir accused. 'The way you bolted in Nice—the way you bolted after we'd made love . . .'

'We didn't make love,' Cathy retorted angrily. 'You forced me, I didn't have a choice. You may not call that rape, maybe you prefer a nicer name for it, but you know I'm telling the truth this time—you made me give in to you. You held me down on the floor and took me and ignored everything I said.'

There was a dark red stain on his cheeks and his eyes leapt with rage. 'You wanted me! Okay, I forced the issue, but I had to make you admit the truth about how you felt, and one minute later you'd stopped protesting and you were responding the way I knew you would, because you wanted me, whatever you said to Telford, whatever lies you've told yourself.'

'I haven't lied to myself!'

'No?' His scathing stare told her he did not believe that. 'Then that must be a first, because the way I see it you haven't got the nerve to face up to the truth. That's why you packed a bag and ran. You knew I'd be coming after you and you wanted to put as much distance between us as you could, didn't you? It wasn't Telford you were running away from, it was me. Now why is that, Cathy? Why do I scare you so much you're prepared to leave everything behind you and run like a rabbit?'

Her eyes fell in front of his fixed stare as she tried to pull herself together, trembling. 'I told you, I needed to be alone, I had to work things out. After what's happened my whole life is in pieces—I didn't know what to do, I had to think, and I couldn't do that here.' She had known that if she stayed she would have to face far too many questions from her father, from Mrs Telford and Stephen, she would have to see their faces as they listened, and she had not been able to bear it. She had hurt them, they would be angry with her, and, even worse, there was going to be a lot of talk in Westoak. You couldn't hide anything in a town this size. What had happened was no doubt already a talking point—scandal spread like wildfire here, and Cathy flinched from the idea of being involved in a scandal, especially since she had dragged the Telfords and her father into the public eye. They would hate being whispered about.

'Stop kidding yourself,' Muir said drily. 'You're a coward, and you ran because you couldn't face up to what you'd done.'

'If that's how you want to see it,' she said bitterly, shrugging. He was right, but that didn't make her ready to admit it.

'It wouldn't have done you any good,' Muir told her. 'I'd have come after you and found you, sooner or later.'

She looked up, startled, her green eyes widening

in alarm, and he gave her a mocking, taunting smile.

'We have a score to settle, and I'm not the man to let you get away with what you did to me, believe me!'

She did believe him, her heart hurting as it hammered against her breastbone. 'I swear I lost my memory, Muir—I did! You must believe me—I didn't have any idea that the police suspected you of raping me. They didn't tell me anything about what was going on—ask the Inspector if you won't believe me!'

'I did ask him,' Muir said coolly. 'He backs up your story, but then he would, wouldn't he? You're far too clever to be so obvious as to ask him any questions. Maybe you didn't know they'd charged me, or that the nurse had picked me out at the identity parade—but you knew what you were doing when you pretended to lose your memory, that was deliberate.'

'No!' she protested, shaking her head, and he caught a handful of the soft, golden hair as it swung against her cheek and dragged her head back, moving closer to stare down into her frightened eyes.

'You told them you'd never heard of me, you didn't know my name!'

'I'd forgotten . . .'

'Liar,' he said fiercely. 'You knew what you were doing, don't lie to me! You were opting for Telford and his money.'

'No, that's not true! Stephen's money had nothing to do with the way I felt about him. I was in love with him when we got engaged.'

'But you aren't now,' said Muir, and Cathy's lips stayed open, parted on a reply she couldn't force out.

'You aren't in love with him, you're just determined to marry him because he'll give you all the things you want; a wealthy home, security, status, and on top of that he'll give you something else you want—a husband who won't make too many demands on you. Telford's obviously a nice guy—I could see that. I saw the way he held you and comforted you, more like a brother than a lover—and that's what you want, isn't it? You're not merely a liar, you're a coward, and you haven't got the guts to face up to your own sexuality. You want Telford because you're scared stiff of taking me on.' Muir's voice stopped, but Cathy heard it ringing inside her head, harsh and insistent, making her wince.

'That's not true,' she whispered. 'Any of it. All lies—you're twisting everything!'

'I'm not the one who's twisted!' His face came closer, menace in it. 'Do you know what the sentence is for rape? Five years—with remission, it might whittle down to three. Three years in prison—that was what I had to face, Cathy!'

'I'm sorry, it wasn't deliberate.' He was hurting her, his fingers wound in her hair and dragging on it as he tilted her head. Tears filled her eyes. 'Muir, I swear to you, I didn't lie—I lost my memory, I just didn't remember you.'

His face hardened rather than softening. 'You didn't want to remember me, you mean. You cut me out of your head deliberately, but don't imagine for one instant that you're going to get away with it. You did it so that you could go ahead and marry Telford. Well, you're not marrying him. You're marrying me!'

Cathy's audible gasp of shock made him smile, but it was not a pleasant smile, it was a hard, cold movement of the lips that mocked her.

'I want you to go through some of what I went through in that police station when they told me you'd denied ever meeting me, when they charged me with attempted rape. If I'd seen you then, they'd have had to charge me with murder, because I'd have killed you if I'd got my hands on you!'

She shrank and he smiled at her with icy understanding. 'Oh, don't worry, I've cooled down now—I've seen enough of the inside of a cell to last me for life. No, I can think of more enjoyable ways of punishing you.' He glanced down at her trembling body and a second later she felt his fingertips trail lingeringly from the curve of her breast to her hip. Her breath caught painfully, she pushed his hand away, shaking her head.

'You're crazy! You just told me you wanted to kill me—do you think I'm insane enough to marry you after hearing that?'

'I think you're cowardly enough,' he said drily. 'I think you'll find the alternatives even more unpleasant.' Without haste he put his hand back on her hip, staring into her nervous eyes as he stroked a slow path up towards her breast. 'You haven't thought very clearly, have you? You can't stay in Westoak now and you certainly can't marry Telford. Your name will be mud here after this—believe me, I know what you'll be facing if you try to stay. Any reputation I had was blown to smithereens when I was charged with rape. Even my so-called friends looked sideways at me.'

'I'm sorry,' Cathy sighed wearily. 'Muir, I *am* sorry.'

He ignored that. 'You could get a job elsewhere, of course—but wherever you went, the story would follow you.' He paused. 'I'd make sure of that.' He watched her face whiten and smiled sardonically. 'Had you forgotten the power of the press, my darling? You publicly wrecked my reputation—I'd have no compunction about wrecking yours just as publicly.' He shrugged. 'Unless, of course, you marry me. That would solve both our problems. It will be obvious to everyone that you wouldn't marry me if I'd raped you, in time all the gossip would die down.'

Her mind was in confusion; jostling with unanswered questions, undefined fears. When she stared at him, trying to read his eyes, she was baffled by the gleaming surface of the iris, the enlarged black pupils mirroring nothing but her own face. Then she saw the taut drag of the brown skin across those powerful cheekbones, the carefully reined tightness of his mouth, and a fierce flare of feeling lit inside her.

'Why do you want to marry me if you hate me?' she asked, watching him.

His hand slid from her hair to her throat, his fingertips caressing and yet menacing, moving delicately on her warm skin as though he stroked it but with a tension in his face which carried a distinct threat.

'I want you,' he said. 'And don't confuse sex

with love, Cathy—you killed anything I felt for you when I found out you'd denied you even knew me, but I still want you. Hating you will only make it all the more exciting to know I can have you whenever I want you.'

Her face grew icy cold, her mouth trembled. 'Muir, don't,' she broke out, trying to move back.

The gentle stroking hand at once became a vice, grasping her neck so that she gave a choked cry of pain.

'You're hurting me!'

'Stand still, then.'

Shivering, she obeyed, and he gave her a satisfied little smile. 'That's better. I'll talk to your father tonight and we'll be married as soon as it can be arranged.'

'I won't ...' she began, and felt his fingers tightening round her throat again.

Muir watched her remorselessly. 'Say yes, Cathy.'

She was silent, her eyes restlessly darting away as she tried to think. There was a core of darkness in Muir which she had not suspected when they first met. She had realised that he was a tough journalist whose background made him far more experienced than her own made her; Muir had a charming smile, but there was cynicism in the hard line of his mouth, and his grey eyes could be shrewd and probing. Even so, she had not guessed at the merciless determination to have his own way which had made him force her to make love with him. He had shown her then that he was a man prepared to use force, and his watchful stare told her he would use it again if she didn't do as he wanted.

'You're going to marry me,' he said, his fingers pressing on her neck. She would have bruises there tomorrow, she thought, inconsequentially. 'I won't take no for an answer. Refuse, and I'll print a very full account of my side of the story. You won't have a hole to hide in, Cathy. Everywhere you go, you'll be recognised. I've got a very sexy, cheesecake picture of you in a bikini—remember the snaps I took of you on the beach at Nice? That alone would make my story front page stuff.' He smiled down at her insultingly, his gaze slipping with narrow-eyed amusement over her body, and she felt a wave of hot colour sweeping up her face.

'You couldn't!'

'You'd better believe it,' he said softly. 'I'd destroy you, darling.'

What else would he do if she gave in and married him? Cathy thought with sick desperation. She would be at his mercy, trapped in a hell she only guessed at but glimpsed fitfully in those icy grey eyes, and Muir would have no hesitation about hurting her to the very limit of human endurance. She had hurt him, rejected him, left him facing the possibility of a long prison sentence for a crime he had not committed—and the fact that she had not consciously meant to do any of that would not weigh with Muir at all. He wanted revenge, and he meant to get it.

'You have no real choice, do you?' he said with dry satisfaction, and Cathy gave a long, weary sigh of admission. He was right, she had no real choice. If he printed that story, it wouldn't only be her who suffered the consequences—Stephen would wince at them, too, and she had hurt Stephen enough. She could not face the thought of adding to the injuries she had done him.

'Do I gather that meant yes?' Muir murmured, watching her face, and she nodded, her lashes lowered to hide her eyes while she thought. She was going to have to learn how to hide her feelings, her thoughts, from him and so far she did not seem to have had much success.

'Very wise,' he said, then the doorbell went and they both stiffened. Muir muttered something short and fierce, then asked: 'Who's that? Your father?'

He had released Cathy in the surprise of hearing the bell, so she walked unsteadily to the window and glanced out, her face surprised as she recognised who stood on the path.

'It's a friend of mine, Jennie Wilkinson—she works in the firm. She'll have seen the car outside, she'll know I'm at home. I'll have to answer the door.'

Muir frowned impatiently and shrugged. Cathy walked away, paused in the hall and ran a trembling hand over her dishevelled hair before she opened the front door.

'Gone deaf, have you?' Jennie asked, walking past her. 'I've been ringing that bell for five minutes. Where were you? In the loo?' She didn't stop for an answer, she walked into the sitting-room while Cathy was shutting the front door, and Cathy heard her surprised voice say: 'Oh, hello! I didn't realise Cathy had visitors.'

'Visitor,' corrected Muir in a lazy smiling voice. 'I'm in the singular.'

'You certainly are,' Jennie agreed, laughing. 'Don't tell me Cathy's been keeping you up her sleeve?'

Cathy walked into the room and caught a mocking smile on Muir's face. 'Haven't you told your friend about me, Cathy?'

Angry and flushed, Cathy murmured an introduction and Jennie's myopic eyes narrowed as she stared at him. 'Muir Ingram?' A startled look came into her face. She took a hurried step backwards, looking at Cathy. 'What's he doing here?'

'I see my reputation has gone before me,' remarked Muir with a grimly unamused smile.

'What's going on, Cathy? Would you like me to ring the police?' Jennie was keeping a wary eye on Muir, shifting in Cathy's direction imperceptibly as she spoke.

'Nothing is wrong,' Cathy said unsteadily. 'I'll explain later—it's very complicated.'

Muir laughed and Cathy gave him a brief, bitter look. 'I've had enough for one day. Will you go now? We'll talk tomorrow.'

'Tomorrow we'll be on our way to London,' Muir told her coolly, and she heard Jennie give a quick, incredulous gasp.

'I can't leave tomorrow——' she began to protest, desperately seeking some way out, some chance to delay things, and Muir's sardonic stare told her that he perfectly comprehended what was going on inside her head.

'You were ready to go today,' he mocked. 'I see no point in delaying, do you? In fact, I'd say the sooner you left Westoak the better—for you.' His smile held a lazy threat and Cathy accepted, with a sinking heart, that she had no alternative but to fall in with his plans. He was right, of course—the sooner she left the better, not only for herself, but for everyone.

'We'll be leaving immediately after breakfast,' said Muir, then turned towards Jennie, one brow shooting upwards in quizzical amusement, as he saw her wary, suspicious expression. 'I don't bite,' he assured her. 'Despite rumours to the contrary.'

'You seem to bark, though,' Jennie observed, moving even closer to Cathy as though to protect her.

'When the occasion demands,' he agreed.

'You're a man who believes in fitting the mood to the occasion, are you?' Jennie asked, and he laughed, the faint lines around his eyes crinkling and giving Cathy a sharp sense of *déja vu*—that was how he had looked the day she met him, with sunlight on his smiling face. If she had had any inkling of what the future held she would never have smiled back, never have got into conversation with him. Life would be so much easier if you could see the future, she thought grimly, but then perhaps most people would prefer not to know what was ahead of them.

Glancing at his watch, he said: 'I'll be on my way. I'll pick you up at nine tomorrow, Cathy—be here.' The last two words were accented softly, but the look which came with them carried sufficient emphasis for her to get the point, and to make sure she did he added even more gently: 'Remember the power of the press.'

A moment later he had gone, the door closed

sharply behind him, and Cathy felt herself sag with relief and exhaustion like a runner at the finishing line. She sat down in the nearest chair, feeling Jennie's gaze on her.

'What,' Jennie demanded, 'is going on around here?'

'It's a long story,' Cathy sighed. 'Could you do with a drink? I could—I've never felt I needed one in my life before, but I need one now. I wonder if my father still has some whisky? Did Muir leave any?' She was talking in a high, tense little voice like a frightened child, and Jennie stared at her anxiously.

'Cathy, I thought the man who ... who broke in here was Muir Ingram?'

'He didn't break in,' said Cathy. 'I let him in, and I wasn't raped—well, not technically, I suppose that would depend on your definition of the word rape—there are rapes and rapes. I think I will have some whisky. On second thoughts, I'd better not—my father would have a fit.'

'Are you okay!' Jennie asked, her face alarmed.

'I'm just fine.' Cathy closed her eyes and felt her head throb with anguished fever. Everything felt so unreal, she did not know where she was any more—indeed, she did not know who she was or what was happening to her, she was adrift on a fast-running river whose tide was carrying her far away from everything she had ever known, and she had no compass with which to chart her voyage. She was in love with a man who hated her and intended to hurt her, and every instinct of self-preservation and common sense urged her to run before it was too late, yet she knew it was useless to try to escape because Muir had meant that threat. He would print the story if she fled, and Cathy could not let him do that, but at some even deeper level of her mind she knew there was far more to her decision than that.

'Here, drink this,' said Jennie, and Cathy's eyes opened. She found Jennie bending over her with a glass of whisky in her hand.

'I was only kidding, I don't like whisky.'

'Like it or not, you need it.' Jennie eyed her closely. 'You look terrible, if you don't mind my saying so.'

'Would it make any difference if I did mind?' Cathy smiled wryly as she took the glass and sipped the pale golden liquid, grimacing. It hit the back of her throat like swallowed fire, making her cough.

'Wow!' she exclaimed. 'That beats tomato juice, but I don't think I'm likely to get addicted.'

'I wouldn't advise it,' Jennie said, smiling. 'It never works to make a habit of looking for courage at the bottom of a glass of whisky.' She removed the empty glass and sat down in another chair. 'Now, are you going to tell me all about it or shall I just guess?'

'I met him in Nice, he's a journalist, he was attending the conference to report it,' Cathy told her. 'I wasn't wearing my ring—I'd lost the middle stone, remember? It was at the jeweller's and it never occurred to me to tell Muir I was engaged at first—it never came up.' She met Jennie's eyes defensively. 'Well, one doesn't go around saying to everyone: Oh, by the way, I'm engaged, in case you're interested. Normally, they spot the ring, of course.' She met Jennie's eyes amd groaned in self-accusation. 'No, you're right—I should have told him.'

'Did I say something?' Jennie looked around as though to appeal to witnesses. 'Did I utter a word?'

'I know what you were thinking.'

'No, darling, that's your guilty conscience,' Jennie informed her. 'So, when did you break the news to him?'

Cathy told her the rest in a flat voice and Jennie listened without showing what she was thinking, her dark eyes lowered.

'He doesn't believe I lost my memory,' Cathy ended. 'He thinks I lied, I was just pretending to have forgotten.'

There was a silence for a moment and Cathy asked: 'Jennie, do you take my word for it—I *did* have amnesia!'

'I'm prepared to give you the benefit of the doubt, convenient though it obviously seems, but I can see why Mr Ingram might be somewhat narked with you.'

'I'm going to marry him,' Cathy said jerkily.

'What?' Jennie sat up, her face staggered. 'What about Stephen? No, forget I asked that, stupid of me. Cathy, are you sure you're doing the wisest thing? That guy did not look to me like a man who forgave and forgot.'

'No, I don't think he plans to do that,' Cathy said with bitter irony.

'Does your father know about this?'

Shaking her head, Cathy said: 'I'll have to tell him tonight. I'm not looking forward to it.'

'Want me to stay and give you moral support?'

'That's very kind of you, I'm grateful, but I'd better see him on my own.' She changed the subject, trying for a lighter tone. 'Won't Carol be sad to hear that I'm leaving?'

'Desolated,' Jennie agreed, laughing. 'She won't be able to bear it.'

'I wonder if she will get my job?'

'No chance,' said Jennie. 'But if by some horrible stroke of luck she did, I'd start looking for a new job myself. I've had a taste of life with Carol running things, and it was hell!'

Cathy looked at her, eyes stricken, but Jennie did not notice, talking on about the office for another quarter of an hour before she left. Cathy walked to the door with her and stood on the path, feeling the warmth of the late afternoon sunlight soaking into her skin. At this hour of the day there was a serenity in the garden which did not match the troubled emotion inside her; sunlight gleaming on leaf and stone, on the waxen petals of the peonies, showing like dark crimson gouts of blood among their green leaves, on the smouldering purple of foxgloves, the cool white sheaths of lilies with their pollen-laden golden stamens tonguing the air and quivering in every breeze, sending fine showers of dust floating away.

Cathy dreaded having to face her father, she was racked with nerves at the idea of what she would see in his face as he listened, but she was trapped; as much by her own nature as by Muir. He had calculated nicely; using moral and emotional blackmail without a shred of hesitation.

She went back into the house, wishing she had

the courage to risk flight. Would Muir really print that story? She found it hard to believe, except that she couldn't help remembering the ruthless way he had forced her to give in to him the night they made love here in this cottage. What else had that been but a form of rape? However much she had secretly wanted him, however much she had loved him, her own will had refused to make love, she had not wanted to betray Stephen, and Muir had made her do what he wanted. He had pushed aside her scruples, denied her any personal freedom to choose, and taken her. Cathy resented that the more she thought about it. She had been so overwhelmed by guilt and grief over Stephen that she had not stopped until now to think about Muir's behaviour and what it told her about him. One thing it certainly made very clear—Muir would not hesitate to use any methods he had to in the pursuit of his own way.

It was several hours before her father came home. Cathy was in the sitting-room trying to pretend to herself that she was watching television when she heard his car. She got up and switched the set off, her heart in her mouth as she turned to face the door.

His key swinging from his hand, George Winter came into the room and looked at her in a blank way, as though he did not know her, had not expected to see her.

'You're late,' she said brightly.

'I had a visitor,' he said, then he passed a hand over his face in a tired, hesitant way, shaking his head. 'I must sit down, this has been a gruelling day.'

'Can I get you a drink? Do you want your supper now?' Cathy asked, slightly worried by his expression.

'Sit down, Cathy,' her father said, sinking into his usual chair and leaning back with his eyes closed. He looked pale and worn and Cathy walked unsteadily to a chair and sat down, too, a pulse beating at her temples.

'Stephen rang me,' George Winter told her, and she gave a low gasp. 'When I'd heard what he had to say, I was on my way home to talk to you, when Mr Ingram arrived.'

'Muir?'

'Yes.' George Winter was silent for a moment, his eyes opening. Cathy couldn't meet that look, she had lost every shred of colour, she stared down at her hands where they twisted helplessly in her lap. She was afraid of her father, but she loved him, and she couldn't bear to see the look she knew she would find in his face.

'I don't know what to say to you, Cathy,' her father said after a while. 'I wish I could say I understood, but I don't. I thought you really cared for Stephen. I respect and admire Stephen more than anyone I know. He's a splendid young man, I don't know how you could do this to him.'

It was so distressing to hear his weary, quiet voice that Cathy couldn't look up, couldn't even try to speak, even if she had had anything to say. There wasn't anything she could say, though. She had betrayed Stephen, and her father was right.

'When I thought you'd been raped I found it too painful to think about,' George Winter told her. 'I can't tell you how I felt, Cathy. I'd have killed

Ingram if I hadn't kept a tight grip on myself. I suffered for you, I thought nothing worse than that could ever happen to me again. I was wrong. This is far worse—knowing that you . . .' He broke off, his voice harsh, and got up. 'No, I can't talk to you. I don't want to be unkind and I believe Mr Ingram when he tells me you were agonised about walking out on Stephen, but I'm too upset to discuss it further. I'm going to bed. Goodnight, Cathy.'

She heard him walk out of the room, heard his slow footsteps on the stairs, the quiet closing of his bedroom door, and it seemed to her to close on everything that had been her world until today. Her life in Westoak was over and she had nothing to look forward to but marriage to a man who meant to hurt her as much as he could. During her amnesia her mind had been struggling to make a choice between Muir and Stephen, between the past and the future; and she had not been able to commit herself to either, she had been aching with unresolved doubts. Now she saw that in hesitating for so long she had somehow lost both of them. Her relationship with Stephen was over irrevocably, and Muir would never forgive her for that fatal hesitation.

Muir was a man of fierce certainty and assurance—he had known he wanted her and been sure he loved her, he would never forgive her for failing to come up to his personal standard.

CHAPTER SEVEN

It was the middle of the following afternoon when Muir turned into a tree-lined London street which rose steeply in front of them; the flickering shadows of the trees dancing on sunny pavements. Cathy stared out at the large Victorian semi-detached houses on either side of the street.

'Is this where you live?' she asked.

'Where *we* live,' Muir corrected mockingly, giving her a smile that sent the colour rushing to her hairline. He had barely spoken to her on the drive from Westoak, sitting calmly beside her behind the wheel, only the light drumming of his fingertips betraying any sign of impatience as they crawled behind an apparently endless line of other cars driving into London. He had not told her where he intended her to stay, but she had guessed he meant her to stay at his flat, and the prospect had made her highly nervous.

Drawing up outside a high-gabled black and white building, he switched off the engine and watched Cathy glancing at the windows, her brows pleated.

'The ground floor,' he said drily. 'On the left of the door.' Getting out of the car, he slammed his door, walked round to the boot and got out her case. Cathy opened her own door and got out, her pulses skipping as she found Muir standing a few feet away, watching her, his grey eyes glinting as they observed the shapely length of leg exposed by the upward drag of her skirt.

'Ready?' he drawled, and she did not like the way he said it, but she nodded, following him as he walked up the path to the front door. Muir opened it and waved her through into the house. He came inside, closed the door and glanced at a table which stood against the cream-painted wall of the wide hall. A pile of letters were arranged on the table top. While Muir picked up several of them, Cathy watched sunlight flowing through the stained glass panels in the front door, the vivid red and green of the glass reflected in shimmering pools on the floor. A flight of stairs led upwards from the hall, their treads covered in dull beige carpeting. On the ground floor she saw several doors with numbers on them. Holding his letters, Muir turned and walked across to one on the left, unlocked it and looked at Cathy over his shoulder.

'This is it. My income doesn't run to a luxury flat—if that's what you were expecting!'

'I wasn't expecting anything!'

'Just as well,' he said as she walked slowly into the narrow little corridor beyond him. Muir went ahead of her, carrying her case, and she stayed on his heels, halting as she watched him walk into a bedroom. Comfortably furnished, and quite large, it was dominated by a kingsize bed with a heavy cream woven coverlet. Floor-length dark blue curtains hung at the windows; a pleasant but unexciting cream paper which had a raised pattern of slightly metallic stripes covered the walls. While Cathy threw a hurried, nervous look around the room, Muir put down her case and turned back towards her. She shot away from the door and went into the room beyond, relieved to find herself in a small sitting-room.

When Muir loomed up behind her she stammered: 'Where's the kitchen?'

'Need a compass?' he asked, raising one brow, then walked over to the couch which took up a large part of the room and threw himself on to it. 'I'd like a cup of tea, if that's what you plan on making.' Ignoring her, he opened one of the letters he held, and Cathy looked at his profile, biting her lip, before she went out to explore the rest of the flat.

There wasn't much to explore: a modern, green-tiled bathroom with a shower cubicle and next to that a narrow kitchen with a small window which overlooked the house next door, between the two houses only a wooden fence, some dusty-looking lilac trees and a row of plastic dustbins. It was not an inspiring view.

Cathy filled the kettle, put it on and started opening cupboards. The kitchen was well equipped and everything was very neat. Did Muir pay someone to come in and do his housework? Or did he keep the place tidy himself?

They had not discussed what Cathy was expected to do after they were married. She had no idea what to expect about her wedding, either. Muir had told her that it would be a brief civil ceremony, that was all. Her father had not suggested that he might come to it, she would have nobody there, it would hardly be a wedding of any kind. She winced as she remembered the wedding she had planned with Stephen: the long white dress, the veil, the flowers and organ music, the bridesmaids and large reception. This was not how she had imagined being married, this rapid hole-and-corner ceremony in a strange city among total strangers. She felt disorientated, isolated, lost.

What was she going to do with herself every day while Muir was at work? Obviously it would only take a few hours each week to keep this small flat tidy—she couldn't occupy herself full-time with housework.

When she had made the tea she carried a laden tray into the sitting-room and found Muir watching cricket on the television, his hands linked behind his head and his lean body lounging casually against the couch cushions. Cathy put the tray down on a low, leather-topped coffee table, conscious of the fact that he watched her every movement. She poured him a cup of tea and passed it to him before pouring one for herself. Muir's grey eyes derisively observed her as she sat down on a chair on the other side of the room.

'I'm going to get a job,' Cathy announced abruptly, her eyes on her cup.

'Resigned from Telfords yet?' he asked without commenting on her decision, and she nodded.

'I wrote to Mrs Telford last night and posted the letter early this morning. I can hardly ask her for a reference, though.'

'I might be able to get you a secretarial job on the paper,' Muir suggested, and she looked up in surprise. She had expected him to make difficulties, not offer to help, and he read her expression with a crooked little smile.

'I'm not a millionaire, I can't afford to keep you

in luxury and idleness,' he drawled, then the grey eyes became polished steel slits. 'I'm not Stephen Telford.'

Cathy flushed. 'I expect I can find a job in a hotel, I have five years' experience of the hotel business.'

'I'd rather you worked on the paper,' Muir said shortly. 'I want you where I can keep an eye on you.' She stiffened in panic at the look in the grey eyes. 'I wouldn't trust you out of my sight,' Muir ended, staring at her.

She felt a nervous, trembling sensation deep inside her and kept her eyes down, avoiding that look, but through her lashes she could see the implacable line of his mouth: hard, dominating, ruthlessly determined. Breathing rapidly, she fought to keep her alarm out of her face.

The phone rang and Muir swore, moving off to answer it with a lithe grace she watched with an ache of longing. 'Yes? What the hell do you want?' he snarled at whoever was on the other end of the line. 'No, I can't ...' He broke off, forehead creased. 'When? How bad is it?' She heard him whistle softly. 'What about our local stringer? Who is it?' Another pause, during which she heard a distant, indistinguishable voice talking fast. Muir broke in: 'Send Tom Mayes—what? How in God's name did he manage to do that? Surely you've got someone else who could go? Barry, I'm not putting up with this!' The voice interrupted him and he listened, scowling broodily at the window. 'Okay,' he said, 'I'll be over there in half an hour.'

Cathy watched him slam the phone down. Turning, he surveyed her with a moody impatience.

'I've got to leave, that was the paper. There's been a bad train crash in Kent, they want me to get down there right away. No idea when I'll be back. There's plenty of frozen food in the deep-freeze—make yourself at home.' He crossed the room at a stride and Cathy involuntarily backed out of the way, getting a hard, angry look.

'And you can stop jumping every time I come anywhere near you!' He came close, a hand lifting to push the hair back from her throat. Cathy stiffened as he bent and kissed the exposed skin with lingering deliberation. 'It makes me want to hurt you,' he said very softly. His teeth grazed her lobe, bit delicately, making her flinch.

'I said don't do that,' Muir warned. 'If I hurt you, it will be because you've asked for it.' He closed his fingers around her wrist, jerked her arm up behind her back and used it as a lever to bend her backwards over his arm. Pale, uncertain, she didn't dare to struggle, and Muir looked at her mockingly.

'What sort of imagination have you got, Cathy? Vivid, is it?'

She didn't answer, but her eyes widened and he smiled with an angry amusement. 'I'd never thought of myself as a sadist. I can't remember ever wanting to hurt someone the way I want to hurt you. They used to leave me alone for an hour at a time in the police station. I had nothing to occupy my mind but you—I thought about you all the time, Cathy, and my imagination worked overtime.' His fingers tightened and she gasped, her skin icy cold with fear. 'You can't imagine what pleasure it would give me to see you cry,' he said huskily, and her lashes dewed with sudden tears, as though he had conjured them up from her. She kept her eyes down, but she knew he watched the slow trickle of moisture and she heard him breathing sharply.

Bending closer, he trailed his tongue across the wet lashes, then before she could catch her breath he was kissing her fiercely, angrily: her lips forced apart, her mouth invaded, plundered, in a kiss which was more an act of bitter possession than anything resembling tenderness or even passion.

A moment later he pushed her away. 'Don't go out,' he said tersely. 'Stay in the flat. Do you hear?'

Cathy nodded, unable to speak, and he walked out. The door slammed and she looked around the sitting-room, her eyes desperate, but there was no way out for her. For the next hour she paced the room, backwards and forwards, with the meaningless activity of a caged animal, trying to think. How was she going to stand living with a man who hated her? Muir had told her he was not going to make her life very pleasant, but she had not expected him to take a sadistic delight in hurting her physically. There had been an element of icily controlled violence in the way he held her, kissed her. She had a numb suspicion that that had only been the tip of the iceberg—Muir's hostility towards her was all the more lethal for being held on such a very deliberate rein.

The white telephone began to ring again and after a moment's hesitation she went over to pick it up. 'Hallo?'

'Cathy?' The voice was tentative, but she

recognised it at once and her hand tightened around the phone.

'Stephen? How did you know I was here?'

'Your father gave me the number. How are you?'

She was very glad he could not see her face, it made it possible for her to fake a cheerful voice. 'Fine! How are you?' She winced as she asked that, feeling like a crass insensitive idiot, but the question had come out involuntarily. Stephen had every right to despise her, to hate her for asking him that.

Instead he said gently: 'I'm okay, Cathy,' and she knew that the words were intended to convey far more than a simple reassurance about his health. 'Your father tells me you're going to marry Ingram.'

'Yes.' It cost her a great deal to answer, she was screwed up inside, her body as taut as a bowstring.

Stephen waited a moment, then said: 'When?'

'In a week.'

She heard a faint sigh, then Stephen said: 'I hope you'll be very happy, Cathy. You know that. I'm always here if you need me. Keep in touch.' The phone clicked and he was gone. Cathy slowly fumbled to replace the receiver, not able to see it through the blinding mist of tears. Losing Stephen was like having part of herself ripped away, she was going to miss him intolerably.

When she felt able to talk coherently she rang Jennie at home and asked her if she would find time to drop in and see Stephen the next day. 'Don't tell him I've rung you, make some excuse, but just see how he is, would you? I'm worried about him.'

'Sure, glad to,' Jennie said. 'I'll have news for him—I saw Mrs Telford this afternoon. She sent for me after lunch and I was expiring of curiosity, I couldn't think what I'd done. I wondered if she was going to boot me out, to be frank, but guess what?'

'You've got my job,' Cathy said, her mouth crooked.

'Did she tell you what she was going to do?' Jennie was taken aback.

'No, I'm just a mind-reader,' said Cathy.

'You could have knocked me down with a feather! I couldn't utter for about five minutes.'

'I wonder what Carol thinks about that,' Cathy murmured.

'I can tell you—she's simply livid! She made no bones about it.'

'I can't think why she should feel like that, she's only been with the firm a few weeks and you've been there for years.'

'Hey, do you mind? You make me sound like an old and valued retainer!' Jennie laughed and Cathy felt a pang of nostalgia—she was gong to miss Jennie more than anyone else, except Stephen. 'As for Carol,' Jennie went on, 'she rejoices in a mind which believes that what it wants it's clearly entitled to—she feels I've snitched her job, she more or less said as much to me.'

'What did you say to her?'

'Bug off,' Jennie reported cheerfully.

Cathy laughed. 'I bet Carol loved that!'

'How are you getting on with Muir Ingram

today?' Jennie asked, changing the subject so quickly that Cathy was at a loss for words.

In the end she said: 'Can I take a rain check on that question?'

Jennie was silent for an interval, then said: 'Ring me whenever you need to talk, won't you, Cathy? Don't lose touch. I may need advice on how to cope with Mrs Telford.'

'Glad to, any time,' Cathy promised. 'She didn't mention me, I suppose?'

Jennie sighed. 'She did, actually. Do you really want to hear?'

'That bad?' Cathy tried to sound calm, her lips pale. 'You'd better tell me, or I'll imagine the worst.'

'She was pretty tight-lipped about you, just mentioned that you weren't going to marry Stephen after all, and had resigned—it wasn't so much what she said . . .'

'As how she said it,' Cathy finished for her. 'I'm not her blue-eyed girl any more, if I ever was! I don't think she ever thought I was good enough for her son, you know, I expect she's secretly half relieved, although no doubt she would like to put me through a mangle for hurting Stephen.' She stopped short, sighing. 'Which is only what I deserve,' she added in a level voice.

'If you're in love with someone else that isn't your fault,' said Jennie with a flicker of impatience. 'Stephen wouldn't have wanted you to marry him if you didn't love him any more. Have some sense, for heaven's sake, Cathy! Stop behaving like a tragedy queen and use your head for once. None of us is responsible for our own feelings, we can't help ourselves. It's much better for you and Stephen to find out now that it didn't work between you than for you to marry him and for him to realise the truth too late to do anything but get a divorce. Mrs Telford wouldn't be pleased about that, either. Face the fact—it's just one of those things.'

When Cathy had rung off she wandered around the flat, feeling very lonely. It was an oddly impersonal place, Muir had a great many books and records, but he had few ornaments and no photographs; there was nothing much to reveal his personality except what she could glean from studying his choice of books and music, and that seemed pretty catholic, which indicated a breadth of taste and intelligence but gave her no real inkling about the man himself.

She switched on the television in time to hear the nine o'clock news. The train crash was the lead story and Cathy watched with distress, relieved to find that there had been no deaths in the accident, although a number of people had been taken to hospital suffering from serious injuries. Rescue workers were still busy on the scene and she decided that Muir might not come back at all that night—the story was obviously still a major news lead, he would probably be kept in Kent for hours.

Switching off the set, she went into the kitchen and made herself some scrambled egg, then had a shower and went to bed. She was so exhausted that she fell asleep almost at once, and slept so deeply that when she woke up she was covered in perspiration and felt hot and shaky, as though she had a temperature. It was almost dawn, the light was stealing through the curtains and she could hear birds beginning to give sleepy cries somewhere among the rooftops.

She fumbled her way into the bathroom, wide awake and wondering when Muir would return. There was no sign that he had come back to the flat during the night. Stripping off her nightie, she stepped into the shower and turned on the jet, sluicing the perspiration from her hot skin, from the lank strands of her blonde hair.

A few moments later she padded back into the bedroom in her short blue towelling robe. Her hair was still wet, plastered to her skull, the colour dark with water. She rubbed it vigorously with a towel, sitting on the edge of the bed, then untied the belt of her robe and let the garment slide off as she turned to pick up her panties. Her arm stiffened without completing the gesture as she found herself looking straight at Muir. He must have come back while she was in the shower, she thought with stunned comprehension. She wouldn't have heard him with the water running full volume.

He wasn't moving, his stare leaping over her smooth-skinned nudity: the pale brown of her hollowed shoulders, the high, firm breasts whose nipples darkened and hardened under his eyes, the flat, tanned midriff, the soft curve of belly and hip and the long slim legs. She heard the harsh intake of his breath and her body burned briefly, in shock, in a fierce sensual excitement, then her hand shot to grab up her robe and she turned her back, hurriedly putting it back on.

She felt rather than heard Muir move. His arms went round her, pulling her back against him, his hands slid inside the robe, and she gave a gasp of protest as she felt them cup her breasts, his long fingers possessive, the warm palms pressing upward into her flesh.

Cathy was facing the mirror, which reflected them both. Her eyes nervously avoided the image of herself; her robe lying open and Muir's caressing hands very brown against her pale skin. Meeting his eyes, instead, she said: 'You must be tired, have you been working all night?'

'Yes,' he said, his chin resting on her shoulder, then turned his face to kiss the damp skin of her throat. 'Cathy,' he muttered into it, and she shuddered, her eyes closing, her body weak with pleasure at what his hands were doing. From her breasts they voyaged slowly, softly, following the silky curve of her body down to the rough triangle of hair. One slipped between her trembling thighs to touch her with a tormenting intimacy which made her lips part on a stifled moan.

She was half aching for him to make love to her, half afraid of how he would do it—the bitter cruelty he had shown her before he went to the newspaper that afternoon had been a warning, Cathy wasn't able to forget what he had said about wanting to hurt her.

To distract him, she said: 'You must be hungry, can I get you some breakfast?' and Muir laughed, but without real humour, he sounded angry.

'I don't want food, I want you. You know that.' He made it sound like an accusation, his voice biting, and as she tried to move away he snarled, a harsh animal sound which seemed to break from him almost without his being aware of it. 'I said I want you!' Cathy froze, terrified, her white skin stretching around her eyes in a mask of fear, then he pushed her backwards on to the bed and knelt beside her, looking down into her face, watching the emotions she could not hide.

'I told you, whenever I want you, I'm going to have you.' He kissed her with such insistence that she thought she would suffocate, her head clouding and her ears beating with blood. He sat up and she lay there weakly, too dazed to move, hearing him pulling off his clothes in a haste which was underlined by the quick, thick sound of his breathing. A moment later he was lying beside her, kissing her throat, his hands touching her with possessive desire, and Cathy's body began to tremble violently as she felt the rough, muscled thigh move against her own. A piercingly intense sensation thrust through her, she wanted him too much to care any longer if he meant to hurt her, when he kissed her mouth it opened to his searching, demanding kiss, her arms locking round his neck.

Muir reluctantly lifted his mouth, but only to kiss her neck and then her breasts, one hand gently stroking the warm flesh curving downward to her thigh. His mouth moved downward too in a seductively coaxing exploration, kisses which brushed over her skin and left her moaning with increasing passion, her hands reaching for the black head as it descended, her mind forgetting everything but the gentle incitement he was inflicting.

'Muir!' Her own voice sounded high and faint,

she heard it echoing inside her skull, reverberating from her taut bone structure.

'Do you love me?' he whispered hoarsely, and she moaned: 'Yes, I love you, I love you,' knowing that at that instant he could have made her say anything, do anything; her whole body was his prisoner, slavishly obedient to his slightest wish. She had never imagined a pleasure like the one he was giving her; the savage cruelty she had been expecting had no point of contact with this, every movement of his mouth made her whimper and tremble, burning with the need for satisfaction.

Muir slid up over her, their bodies glazed with heat, their skins so moist with perspiration that she felt them clinging wherever they touched.

'Look at me, Cathy,' he said in that husky, uneven voice, and she was reluctant to open her eyes, she did not want to let anything break into the intensity of feeling which seemed to wall them off from the rest of the world. 'Look at me,' Muir insisted, his hand taking her chin. 'I want to see your eyes.'

Slowly, her lashes lifted, she looked at him dazedly, her mouth quivering with aroused desire.

'Now tell me the truth—did you have amnesia or were you lying?'

The bitter question tore into her like a knife and she felt herself stiffen in pain and shock. It was the last thing she had expected him to say, it destroyed the melting happiness of her mood just as much as if he had struck her in the face.

When she didn't speak, he looked at her, his eyes dark with hatred. 'Answer me, damn you!'

Her throat ached with the salt of unshed tears,

she shook her head, whispering: 'I was telling the truth. Muir, I . . .'

'You had to choose between me and Telford and you chose him,' Muir insisted, overriding the last word and she blindly shook her head.

'No!'

'Oh, yes,' he said. 'Don't lie to me, never lie to me again, Cathy. I'll get the truth out of you if I have to twist it out with my bare hands.'

'Why should I lie . . .' she began, and he laughed.

'Why?' The jeering note in his voice made her wince, his mouth was icily mocking. 'You've been engaged for two years to a man who's been too ill to do more than give you a kiss or two—when we met, you must have been as frustrated as hell. You wanted me, but you didn't want to lose Telford and his money, did you?'

'That's not true!'

'I say it is,' Muir grated. 'You wanted to have your cake and eat it, too, didn't you? When you got caught out, you lied to stop Telford finding out you didn't love him. I was a stupid fool, I thought that if we made love and you had to admit the way you felt about me you would realise you couldn't marry Telford, but that wouldn't have been the way it happened, would it? If you hadn't fallen, if your father hadn't come back when he did, you'd have sent me off back to London, telling me you didn't want to see me again.'

Cathy looked at him, shrinking from the contemptuous light in his eyes, shaking her head but unable to speak.

'You were just going to give me my marching

orders when you fell,' he went on, as if compelled.
'I'd given you all you needed, all you wanted from
me, hadn't I? You'd even been clever enough to
make me force myself on to you, so that you
wouldn't need to tell yourself you were guilty of
anything! You provoked me into taking you; you
admitted you loved me but refused to break off
with Telford, refused even to see me if I waited for
months for you. You knew what you were doing
all along. You wanted me to force you so that you
could go on telling yourself you weren't to blame.
I heard you, remember, telling your father that
you hadn't wanted to do it, I'd made you. That
was when you betrayed me. All the rest—the
police, the rape charge—that was accidental. But
you betrayed me and you always meant to—even
if you hadn't fallen, if your father hadn't come
back, the end result would have been the same.
You would have loaded all the guilt on to me and
sent me away.'

'No,' Cathy whispered, but inside her head a
little voice kept asking: was it true? It hadn't
looked like that to her, from her side of their
relationship, but was there some truth in his
accusation all the same? Seen from outside, by a
neutral observer, might Muir's bitter accusations
have the ring of truth? She had wanted him, that
was true, she had been achingly in love with him,
and she had admitted it that night. When he made
love to her she had stopped fighting after a few
moments, if she had been taken by force she had
been a very willing victim. Truth was never black
and white, it was a grey cat walking in shadows.
Cathy couldn't see it clearly enough to be sure

how much of what Muir had said had come anywhere near the truth.

'You lied when you pretended to have amnesia, didn't you?' he demanded.

Cathy didn't answer, ice-cold with anguish.

'Answer me! You lied, didn't you? Admit it, you were only pretending to lose your memory.' His eyes had a savagery that wanted to hurt, she looked away from them, shivering. 'How do you think I felt once that dawned on me? How do you think it felt to be used like that, manoeuvred into the position of a scapegoat, loaded with all the responsibility, all the guilt, so that you could drive me out afterwards once you'd finished with me?'

'No, it wasn't like that, that's not true!'

'It's the truth. I was crazy about you, I thought you were the eighth wonder of the world, and you were just a ruthless amoral bitch who took what she wanted and then kicked me in the teeth. I thought I knew all there was to know about women, but boy, was I wrong! You've taught me a whole new textbook on the subject. You're such a liar you even lie to yourself, but you aren't lying to me again and getting away with it. I want the truth from you, starting now. You lied, didn't you? You didn't have amnesia?'

'No,' Cathy half sobbed, then she broke down entirely, sobbing out a muffled denial. 'No, no, no, I forgot, I forgot—I felt guilty and ashamed and I forgot, but it wasn't deliberate, I wasn't pretending!'

'You felt guilty, that much I buy, but you remembered,' Muir said scathingly, watching her with remorseless eyes. 'You didn't forget me, that

I'll never believe, so you can get this straight, Cathy—sooner or later you're going to admit the truth. Save yourself a lot of pain. Admit it—because until you do I'm not going to let up. I'm going to make you admit it. We won't have any sort of marriage until you do.'

She lay there, staring blankly at him, and he smiled tightly at her. 'You want me, we both know that. You were almost begging for it just now, but you aren't going to get it until you've admitted you were lying when you said you'd forgotten me. I'll see you climbing the walls before I lay a hand on you again—until you've told the truth. I'm not starting a marriage with that sort of foundation—I'd never be able to believe a word you said.'

He got off the bed and walked towards the door. Struggling with tears, Cathy stared at the long, graceful lines of his naked back, the smooth brown shoulders gleaming in the morning light. As he went out he said: 'I'm going to have a shower and get dressed—get me some breakfast, will you? I have to go into the office.'

The door closed quietly and Cathy brushed a shaking hand over her tear-stained face, sniffing like a beaten child, her mind wincing at the future Muir had just outlined for her.

CHAPTER EIGHT

IT was several minutes before she felt able to move, then she wearily got up and dressed and went into the kitchen. As she filled the coffee percolator she heard Muir leave the bathroom and go into the bedroom. He closed the door, and Cathy hurriedly splashed her face with cold water and dried it roughly before she set about getting the breakfast. She cooked egg and bacon and squeezed some oranges, laid the table in the sitting-room by the window, and was just taking the coffee into the room when Muir emerged. Cathy turned her head to avoid his eyes, but as they sat opposite each other she felt the sardonic, watchful gaze moving over her, reading her face as though Muir knew everything which was going on inside her.

'I spoke to Barry last night about finding you a job on the paper,' he said as he put some marmalade on his toast. 'He says there's a vacancy in the advertising department, if you'd like to try that.'

Cathy kept her eyes on her coffee. She had not been able to eat anything, but Muir had had no such problem, he had apparently enjoyed every mouthful of his egg and bacon and was now demolishing the rack of toast.

'If you want the job Barry will fix an interview for you some time tomorrow with the advertising manager,' Muir added. 'Shall I tell them you're interested?'

'Yes, please,' she said. At least she would not be in the newsroom under Muir's eyes.

He sipped his coffee, nodding. 'Right, I'll get it fixed up.' Glancing at his watch, he got up. 'I'm off, I don't know when I'll be back.' Pulling out a wallet, he laid some notes on the table. 'Will you do some shopping, stock up the larder? Why don't we have some braised liver tonight? I haven't eaten that for years; they rarely have it in restaurants. My mother used to cook it with onions and tomatoes in a sort of Provençale sauce.' His face softened, he was smiling, Cathy couldn't believe it.

'Was your mother a good cook?' she asked tentatively, and he laughed.

'Terrific—she spent hours getting meals. She didn't have a job, of course, her whole life was the home, Dad and myself. I was lucky, I had very young parents. My mother was only twenty when I was born.'

'When did she die?' Cathy asked, and the smile went out of his eyes.

'Six years ago. They were both killed in a plane crash. My father was nuts on planes, he liked to fly in light aircraft. He took a flying course so that he could pilot himself. They didn't have the money to buy a plane, he used to hire one for a few hours at the flying school. He took my mother up one day, she was scared stiff, she hated flying, but he was eager to show her how good he was.' Muir stopped talking, his face sombre. 'There was something wrong with the controls, and they crashed five minutes after taking off.'

'I'm sorry,' Cathy said, wanting to comfort him but not daring to move any closer because although he was talking to her in a level voice she couldn't forget the bitterness and cruelty he had shown her an hour ago.

'I miss them,' Muir said brusquely, and turned on his heel almost before he had finished speaking.

The front door banged, and he was gone. Cathy sat thinking about him for a few moments, then cleared the table, washed up, tidied the kitchen and made the bed. She spent an hour working in the flat, then went out to explore the district. She walked to the top of the steep road and saw a row of shops at the far end of the intersecting road in which she found herself. The morning was clear and bright, the sun sparkled on the chrome of the cars, on windows and gardens, and Cathy had a lazy awareness of summer, of the smell of privet from hedges, newmown grass, flowers. It was not a feeling she had associated with London, but as she walked along the narrow High Street a few moments later, she realised that the area had an oddly village-like atmosphere. Although there were several large supermarkets, there were also many small shops; a butcher, a florist, a paperback bookshop, a modern chemist, with just across the road a very old-fashioned chemist in whose window she saw little piles of dried herbs, ginseng, liquorice root and privately made-up natural remedies.

When she had done her shopping she walked back to the flat behind a girl with a neat black ponytail of hair swinging down her back, who was pushing a canvas pushchair slowly. Cathy saw a pink hand dangling a tattered blue rabbit. Suddenly the rabbit sailed through the air just as a car zoomed towards them. Cathy darted into the road picked up the toy and flashed out of the way as the car screeched past, hooting fiercely. The distracted driver shook an angry fist at her before he vanished.

Cathy restored the rabbit to its beaming owner, whose mother had stopped dead in her tracks, her expression aghast.

'You could have been killed—you're crazy!' she exclaimed. She was barely older than Cathy; thin, fine-boned, with a pair of very bright blue eyes that dominated her face. She wasn't wearing make-up, but she didn't need any, her face was a smooth tanned oval on which cosmetics would have been pointless.

'I'd have hated to see Bunny get ripped to pieces,' Cathy said, laughing.

'Wabbit,' corrected the other girl. 'That's what he calls it. I think it's a love–hate relationship, Joey is always trying to chuck the thing away.'

Cathy looked down on the baby's head. Joey was ignoring them, intent on trying to pull off one of the rabbit's long ears.

'I saw you in the butcher's,' the girl remarked, beginning to walk on, and Cathy fell into step. 'Just moved in? I haven't seen you before. I'm at number twenty, ground floor flat.'

'I'm on the ground floor at twenty-one,' Cathy said, surprised.

'Really? Don't tell me that dishy man with black hair has moved? You've ruined my day!'

Cathy flushed. 'He hasn't moved, no.'

She got a curious, amused look. 'He hasn't moved out but you've moved in?'

'We're getting married,' Cathy said defensively.

'No kidding? Some people have all the luck. I'm Liz Wood, by the way.'

'I'm Cathy Winter.'

Liz smiled at her. 'If you're not too busy, why don't you come in for a coffee? The days sometimes seem to drag, there aren't many young people in this street. My husband doesn't get home until seven and some days I find myself talking like a two-year-old after a day with Joey. It's catching, you know. When Andrew comes in I catch myself saying: 'Din-dins is nearly ready.' I can tell you, he gives me some very funny looks at times!'

'Din-dins?' said Joey, waking up to the fact that interesting subjects were being discussed. He beat the rabbit's head on the arm of his pushchair. 'Din-dins, din-dins!'

'See what I mean?' Liz groaned as she pushed him up the garden path towards the house. Cathy followed, looking sideways.

'Your house is the view I get from my kitchen,' she told her.

'Snap! Inspiring, isn't it? Brick walls and chimneypots. It really makes your heart lift in the early morning.' As she unlocked the front door of her flat Liz said ruefully: 'It's in a mess, I'm afraid—it always is, Joey insists on living in a state of squalor, he's havoc on two legs!'

The sitting-room was furnished in a modern way, there were no ornaments or books on a level which the baby could reach, but the floor was littered with toys. Liz took Joey out of his pushchair and dropped him, kicking and squawking, into a lobsterpot playpen, adding a little shower of toys which she scooped up from the floor.

'Come into the kitchen and talk while I get the coffee,' she said.

Cathy looked back as they left the room and saw the toys whizzing back out of the playpen while Joey chuckled, holding the rim with one hand while he bowled toys with the other.

She stayed for half an hour, but said very little. Liz made up for that, she talked happily about the district, her husband, the neighbours. Walking Cathy to the door, she said: 'See you again, soon, I hope. Drop in for a coffee any time.'

'I'd love to, but you must come to me next time,' Cathy said warmly. It would be fun to have a near neighbour of her own age to talk to, and meeting Liz had made her feel slightly less lost and out of place in this London district.

When Muir returned to the flat he had someone with him. Cathy was in the kitchen, sprinkling herbs over the braising liver, when she heard voices. A moment later Muir appeared in the doorway, leaning there casually with one hand propping him up.

'I brought Barry back with me, I supose there isn't enough liver for three?' His voice sounded relaxed and easy, it carried none of the bitter tension which had lain between them earlier.

'I can stretch it,' said Cathy, and someone standing behind Muir laughed.

'Did he spring me on you? Go on, throw a saucepan at him—I would!'

Muir turned, grinning. 'Cathy, this is my news editor—Barry Loring,' he introduced, and the man behind him smiled at her.

'Hi, Cathy.' He gave her a quick once-over with very bright hazel eyes, his thin brows shooting up. 'I've been dying to see the sort of girl who could make Muir throw away his little black book—I might have known she'd be dynamite!'

Cathy laughed, flushing. 'Thank you.' He was a slightly shorter man than Muir, very broad in the shoulder, his head rugged, his hair thick and wiry, the colour of bracken in autumn, a reddish-brown. It curled untidily, cropped close to the side of his head and springing up in a determined way on the top of it. Cathy put his age at nearer forty than thirty, his face had humour in it, but it also had a form of cheerful pugnacity.

'A blonde,' Barry said. 'I should have known she'd be a blonde—this man of yours has always flipped over blondes. Or am I telling tales out of school?'

'*You* are opening your mouth a little too wide,' Muir told him lazily. 'Just watch it, Loring. Come on, I'll get you a drink before you give away any more of my secret past.'

Did he have a secret past? wondered Cathy as the two men walked into the sitting-room. They had never talked about Muir's earlier love life, Cathy had not asked him any questions and he had not volunteered any information. She had taken it for granted that there had been other women before her, it hadn't mattered, but now it did. Now she felt far too conscious of the abyss between them: the unknown, unfathomable depths of Muir's nature from which his violence sprang, that savage reaction to what he saw as rejection. She needed to know all she could about him if she was to find a way of bridging that gulf. His anger over having been suspected of raping her was quite understandable, she bitterly regretted that she had caused such embarrassment and humiliation for him, but that morning she had realised that Muir's rage had not sprung from that. He was angry with her because he thought she had betrayed him, and how could she ever convince him that her betrayal had not been deliberate?

They had dinner at eight o'clock. Cathy had managed to eke out the meal she had planned in order to make it stretch to three, adding another vegetable and some grilled bacon. Muir seemed to enjoy the food, he smiled at her as she served the coffee later and said: 'That was terrific, thank you.'

'Was it anything like the liver your mother used to make you?' she asked, handing him his cup, and Barry chuckled, his expression wickedly amused.

Muir gave him a dry look. 'I'm very partial to braised liver,' he informed Barry. 'And yes, it was similar, but I think she used to put something else in—no idea what. This is delicious, though.'

'I'll second that,' said Barry.

He stayed for several hours after dinner, talking casually, mostly to Muir but often remembering to draw Cathy into the conversation, asking her about her own family, telling her about the sort of work she would do in the advertising department.

'The manager can see you at four tomorrow, is that okay?' he asked, and she nodded.

'Fine. What's his name and where do I find him?'

'His name is MacIntyre and he lives on the third floor—reception will direct you. He'll give you more details of the job, you'll probably have to take a few speed tests, that sort of thing. It isn't a difficult job, just dealing with the advertisers either on the phone or by post. You can do it on your head, I'm sure.' He glanced at his watch. 'I must be going. Look, my wife comes back from Scotland tomorrow and we're having a party on Saturday night—why don't you two turn up, meet the gang? Cathy should get to know us all. My place any time after eight. You can bring a bottle if you're feeling generous, Muir.'

'Okay,' said Muir, and Barry gave Cathy a parting smile before walking off with Muir. The front door closed and Muir came back alone, and in the brief time it had taken him to show Barry out and walk back down the corridor he had undergone a swift change of mood. The smiling, charming man who had sat there for three hours talking to Barry had vanished and in his place Cathy saw the hard-featured, cold-eyed man who had been haunting her all day ever since his bitter attack on her. Her heart sank and her smile withered.

'I'm going to bed,' Muir said tersely. 'I'm dead.'

He was gone, and she stared at the place where he had been, her eyes stricken. She stayed up for another hour, wondering what to do, then at last crept into the bathroom, had a shower and made herself a bed on the couch, with the spare pillow and quilt she had already noticed in the large airing cupboard taking up one wall in the bathroom. She lay awake listening to the murmur of traffic from the streets around her, and it was a long time before she fell asleep.

Muir woke her up with a cup of coffee. He was dressed, his face impossible to decipher in the shadowy morning light. The curtains were still drawn and Cathy tensed as Muir looked down at her. 'I'm just leaving,' he said shortly. 'It's nine o'clock.'

'Oh, sorry, I . . .'

Her words died as he walked away. A moment later she heard him leave the flat and lay with a feeling of dreary misery for company, listening to the birds and the sound of someone in the flat above vacuuming. Why had he insisted that she marry him when he meant to treat her like this? How could he want to be trapped in this love–hate relationship with her? It was going to be hell for both of them, he must be crazy to insist they marry, he was punishing himself as much as her, or did he hate her so much that however much it cost him he was determined to set about systematically destroying her? Last night, while Barry was there, he had been again the Muir she had met in Nice; laughing and swapping anecdotes with Barry, talking with amusement about current news stories or people in the office, describing a play he had recently seen and talking quietly, with feeling, about the scene at the rail crash. That had been the man she loved, the grey eyes had been without a trace of this bitter hostility. How could he switch off and on like that?

That morning Liz came round for coffee and

Joey spread a path of destruction around the sitting-room. 'Don't be silly, he isn't doing any harm,' Cathy assured her as Liz winced when Joey pulled a row of Muir's books out of the bottom shelf and began building a crazy house with them, but Liz went over and detached him, red in the face with fury, to put him back into his push-chair.

'I'll have to get moving, anyway—I've got a pile of ironing to do. See you!' She pushed Joey out of the flat, talking, and when she had gone the silence descended again, like a muffling blanket.

Cathy ate a sandwich for lunch and got ready to have her interview with the Advertising Manager at the newspaper. The building was at the end of Fleet Street, a high tower of glass and concrete whose windows glittered in the afternoon sunshine as Cathy stood on the pavement looking upwards. She walked through the swing doors and the receptionist directed her to the floor she wanted.

Mr MacIntyre was a man in his late middle age; burly, slightly harassed, with thinning brown hair and lines massing on his forehead in serried ranks as though he perpetually frowned. He rose, shaking hands, and gestured to the chair opposite him, scanning her all the time with that worried expression.

'I gather you're just about to marry Muir Ingram?' he asked, and she nodded. 'Have you had any experience of advertising before?'

'In the hotel business, a little,' she said, and outlined her previous career.

'Why are you leaving your present job?' he asked. 'Because you're marrying Muir, I suppose.'

'Yes,' she said, wondering with some apprehension if he was about to question her about the Telford firm, ask her for references, but he merely nodded.

'Of course, your hours will be strictly office hours—you won't be working the same shifts as Muir.' He smiled briefly. 'He works whenever a story is running, but you'll realise that already. There's no such thing as office hours for a journalist.'

Cathy nodded; she had already gathered as much. Mr MacIntyre studied her face, his broad hands on his desk.

'Well, shall we see what you can do? I'll ask you to take some dictation and type a letter first, shall I?'

She left the office half an hour later knowing that she had passed the tests. She had got the job.

Muir arrived home just after eight. Cathy was reading one of his books, a new biography of Liszt which she had picked up casually, thinking how much her father would enjoy it. When she heard the front door open she felt her pulses leap and she struggled to look cool as Muir glanced at her from the sitting-room door.

'Sorry I'm late—I had to drive out to Ipswich to cover a story, I only just got back.'

'I got some steak,' Cathy said. 'It won't take ten minutes to grill—will you have salad with it?'

'Fine,' he said with a politeness which was iced.

Cathy went into the kitchen, hating him. She cooked and served the meal and Muir asked how she had got on with Mr MacIntyre.

'I got the job, I think I'll enjoy working there— the girls in the office seemed very friendly.'

'It's the men you'll have to watch,' Muir said drily, eyeing her through his lashes, and she felt her cheeks glow with heat. 'Advertising men all go for blondes, they're conditioned to drool every time they see one.'

'According to Barry, so are you,' Cathy snapped, and saw his eyes narrow with gleaming amusement.

'You don't want to believe half what Barry says, he's a born troublemaker. Trouble is his middle name, he runs the office by the motto: divide and rule. That way he makes sure any conspiracies start with him and he can squash rebellions before they get under way.'

'I liked him,' Cath said.

'So do I,' Muir drawled. 'But that doesn't mean I don't keep a wary eye on him. He's a pal of mine, but I'm not blind to the fact that he's second cousin to a Borgia prince. He sees a dagger behind every smile and gets in first.'

Her expression made him laugh. 'Look, conspiracy is a way of life in firms like ours. The office is stacked with ambitious men watching for a way to the top. While Barry sits in his chair, nobody else can sit in it—and he knows it, so he's as wary as a farmer with a yard full of chickens and foxes down every hole.'

'You seem to see conspiracy and double-dealing everywhere,' Cathy commented, her eyes feverish.

Muir met her stare, his mouth hardening. 'Are we talking about you?'

'I didn't pretend . . .' she began, and he cut in curtly.

'You did.' He got up and walked out before she

could say any more, and she felt like screaming and stamping her foot to make him listen, to make him believe. When she had washed up and tidied the kitchen she went to bed, hearing Muir moving around in the sitting-room for a while before she finally fell asleep.

When she woke up the room was full of a deepening rosy light and she was alone in the vast bed, yet she immediately knew Muir had slept beside her all night; one of his black hairs lay on the pillow next to her, a pillow which bore the deep impression of his head. Cathy sat up, listening, but didn't hear him, so she lay down again, torn between misery and anger, then rolled across into the faint hollow where his body had lain and nestled her face against his pillow. The bed was cold where he had slept and she felt cold lying in it, cold and lonely, and she continued to feel like that over the next two days.

That Saturday they drove to Barry's house, which was several miles away from Muir's flat, in another London suburb, which looked to Cathy very much the same as the area where Muir lived. The city lay all around them, in circle upon circle; ringed like some vast tree, yet each section complete in itself, leading a busy village life, as if unaware of all the other villages in the spreading circles.

Barry met them at the door, waved them in, giving Cathy an appreciative stare. 'Save me a dance, won't you? Grab a glass and circulate, I'm trying to stop people propping up walls and just chattering to their friends. Muir, if you see Polly around, introduce Cathy, won't you? She's probably in the kitchen slicing quiches.'

'We'll find her,' said Muir, and walked through a noisy mob of people with Cathy at his heels. She got stared at, speculative curiosity in the faces they passed, but as far as she could see the curiosity was all friendly; none of them gave her the sort of look she would expect if they had heard about Muir's arrest, and knew that she had been responsible.

Pushing open a door, Muir said: 'Oh, there you are—Polly this is Cathy, she's eager to help you out, she's very domesticated.'

The woman in the kitchen turned, laughing. Cathy shyly offered her hand and heard the door close as Muir left.

'Did you volunteer, or were you pushed?' Polly Loring asked, and Cathy looked slightly helplessly at her, lost for words. 'Isn't that just like a man? If I were you I'd go after him and pour a glass of whisky down his shirt.'

'He might hit me,' Cathy said with pretended humour, and Polly gave her a grin. Small, very slim, she was in glittery black; a very chic suit with a fringed black top cut low in a vee, and loose pants that matched. Cathy guessed her age at middle thirties and her hair to be originally mousy brown—at present it was hennaed and strikingly styled, layered and very short, close to her head. Her face was clever, lively, very alert, her eyes a warm brown.

'I'd like to help, though,' Cathy assured her. 'What can I do?'

'Nonsense, go and enjoy the party, the press gang isn't operating tonight—at least, not in here, it isn't. I wouldn't say the same for what's going on out there. Mind you, Barry had no difficulty getting volunteers to man the bar. He almost got knocked down in the rush, in fact.' Polly smiled at her. 'Honestly, I've had offers of help and turned them down, I can cope—you're here to enjoy yourself, go on, get a drink and a man and start living.'

'I don't know anyone yet,' Cathy confessed. 'I'd rather stay and talk to you, if you don't mind. I don't know much about Muir's job and his friends yet . . .'

'And you'd like to pick my brains?' Polly surveyed her thoughtfully, brown eyes shrewd. 'Be my guest, to coin a phrase. While we chat you can cut up this cheese into bite-size pieces for me and skewer them with these sticks—there's a bowl of pineapple chunks there, you can stick one of them with each bit of cheese.'

They worked, talking, with Cathy asking questions and Polly answering them. 'How long have I known Muir? Four, five years, I suppose, since Barry took over the newsroom. Muir eats here quite a bit—or did.' She smiled at Cathy wryly. 'You know how it is when your husband has bachelor friends—Muir has got into the habit of coming round for Sunday lunch and sometimes we all go to the theatre or have dinner somewhere along the river. We're a very friendly crowd, you'll like us.' Her eyes laughed and Cathy smiled back. 'Muir isn't the only unmarried man on the staff. Barry brings half a dozen friends to lunch at weekends—we get a few of the girls over too and have a party.'

'It all sounds very social,' Cathy murmured.

'We try and enjoy ourselves. All work and no play—you know the saying. Barry is a social animal, he likes people around, and so do I.' Polly gave her an odd quick look. 'Muir is a very different type, isn't he? He's great fun at a party and of course the girls all flip over him. He's very sexy, very attractive, but there's a lot of Muir battened under hatches, isn't there? You'd know that better than me. He's always struck me as something of a lone wolf. I've often had the feeling he's lonely, but very hard to please. I know several pretty girls who'd give their eye teeth to have his attention, but he's been elusive until now. In fact, I can't remember him dating anyone for more than a few weeks. Barry reckons he moves off before a girl can start planning her trousseau.'

'Is this enough cheese?' Cathy asked, and Polly glanced at the neatly arranged plate, nodding. Cathy found she did not want to hear about Muir and other girls.

'That's fine. There are some bowls of prepared salad in the fridge—would you get them out?' She looked at her watch and groaned. 'The sausage rolls! They'll be incinerated!' rushing to the oven, she whipped out a tray of pastry, sighing with relief. 'Just in time! Another minute and they would have been charred beyond recognition.' She tipped the rolls on to a metal mesh tray to cool and dropped the empty tray into the sink with a clatter.

'Barry was fascinated when Muir came back from Nice with a bad case of love—Muir almost went berserk when Barry sent him off to Dublin instead of giving him a week's leave to visit you,' Polly went on.

'Muir told you about me?' Cathy asked huskily, uncertain how much Polly knew.

'He didn't mention your name, just said he'd met the girl he wanted to marry. Love at first sight, Barry said. He was tickled to death. Muir of all people! And then he had the rotten luck to be suspected of raping some girl—but you'll know all about that, he was visiting you at the time, wasn't he? It must have been a traumatic experience for both of you, you must have been out of your mind.'

'Yes,' Cathy said on a quivering note of shock. What had Muir told them?

'We all gave three cheers when the police picked up the real rapist. Muir was a real clam about what happened to him, mind you. Barry has been trying to get him to write the story for the paper— of course, it's always dodgy reporting rape cases, but so long as no names are mentioned Muir could give the background stuff. He could do a fascinating piece on how it feels to be suspected of rape; the police questioning, the procedures and so on—typical of Muir that he won't do it. He has a stubborn sort of integrity, and I respect that. Barry just gets as mad as fire with him—Barry is about as sensitive as a brick wall at times, much as I love the stupid man.' Walking over to the sink, she washed her hands, saying over her shoulder: 'We deserve a drink, let's go and find one. I'll finish arranging the buffet after that, but first I'll introduce you to a few people.'

Cathy washed her hands and dried them on the

towel Polly offered her, then followed her out of
the modern kitchen into a large, rectangular room
which had been cleared of all furniture and was
full of people. Barry gave them both a drink and
Polly took Cathy round the room, introducing her.
She left a moment later and Cathy found herself
involved in a noisy conversation about the latest
political situation. The talk drifted on to cricket
and then to holidays and back to politics. From
another room came the sound of music and people
drifted from one room to another all the time.

Half an hour later Cathy ventured into the other
room and found it full of people dancing. Muir
was there, with a thin girl in green dungarees and
an eye-boggling orange satin shirt, who was
dancing with her arms around his waist. Muir had
his arms around her and they were talking, almost
nose to nose. Cathy ground her teeth and went
out, taking with her the picture of Muir's hands
resting on the other girl's slender hips. It was not a
picture she liked much.

'Oh, there you are,' said Barry, behind her and
she halted to smile. 'I thought you were going to
dance with me?'

'Love to,' Cathy said promptly.

They danced, talking, and Barry asked if she
thought she was going to like working on the
paper.

'I'm sure I shall,' she said, smiling.

He looked down at her slim figure. 'That's a
very sexy dress.'

'Thank you,' she said demurely, lashes fluttering
at him in teasing deliberation, and heard him
laugh softly.

'Oh, yes, Muir knows what he's doing. You are a very classy lady. Is that hair real? I've never seen hair that colour before; is it blonde or red?'

'It's close to being red-gold, and it is real,' Cathy assured him with another flirtatious smile, aware that Muir was dancing a few feet away and still holding the other girl in a far too intimate way. 'All of me is real,' she added as Barry admired her figure without hiding the fact.

'You shouldn't have told me—I was just looking forward to finding out.'

Cathy lifted her brows. 'Were you, indeed?'

Barry grinned. 'I can dream, can't I? Don't worry, Polly would nail me to the front door if I . . .'

'Mind if I cut in?' Muir said behind him, and Barry stopped talking, his hands dropping to release Cathy. 'Thank you,' said Muir with terse courtesy, and got a double-take from Barry as he moved away, taking Cathy with him, his arm tightly and possessively around her waist. She looked at him with indignation; the tone he had used to Barry had been as grating as the one he often used to her.

He looked at her with brooding eyes, his forehead contracting in a scowl. 'Flirt with Barry like that and it will be all round the office!' he muttered, low enough for her to hear but to make sure nobody else did.

'It didn't mean anything!' she retorted, and he gave her a hard stare.

'It never seems to with you.'

'Now look, Muir . . .' she began, and he interrupted.

'This is no place to have a row. People are watching us.'

'You started it!'

'Shut up and dance,' he muttered, his arm tightening and pulling her closer. Cathy fought with a sense of burning injustice for a few seconds, then surrendered to her own desire to be close to him, aware of the lean body moving beside her, touching her, his cheek against her hair, his hand moving softly, sensuously up and down her spine. They didn't talk, they kept on dancing, hardly aware that anyone else was in the room. Cathy's eyes closed, her body was relaxed and melting, her pulses roared in her ears every time Muir's lips brushed her neck, touched her hair. She couldn't think, could scarely breathe, attentive to every breath he took, every little shift of his body, and she didn't care if she was betraying to him that she was aching to make love, it didn't seem to matter whether he hated or loved her. She didn't care about anything but the sheer sensual intensity of her own feelings, the answering emotion she could feel in him.

They left the party soon after midnight. Barry passed them on their way out and gave them a wicked grin. 'Have a fantastic time!' he said, and Cathy answered, 'Thank you, we did,' before she realised that it had not been a question but a teasing order.

'Mind your own damned business, Loring,' Muir said without heat, and Barry laughed as they went out, shouting after them: 'Isn't love wonderful?' Muir ignored that.

He didn't speak as they drove back to the flat.

His profile had a taut line, his body poised in a controlled tension, and Cathy felt herself trembling as she got out of the car and walked up the path. Inside the flat she gave him a nervous glance.

'Shall I make some coffee?'

He was taking off his jacket, staring at her. He shook his head, the grey eyes holding an expression that sent the restless shudder of fever running through her.

He came slowly towards her and her mouth went dry. She couldn't take her eyes off him; watching him with hypnotised stillness, her pupils enormous, lustrous, giving the green eyes the glazed brilliance of intense arousal.

Muir held that stare, his nostrils flaring as he drew in air, his breathing audible. His hand went round her, she heard the zip of her silky red dress hiss, then the material slithered down her body, clinging to her perspiring skin, the crackle of static electricity making her jump. Still staring down into her eyes, he hooked a finger under one of the straps of her red slip and drew it down her arm, then slowly did the same to the other strap. Her slip peeled off inch by inch and her nerves screamed. She knew he was tormenting her, watching her to read her reactions, and she struggled to hide them, knowing she couldn't, there was no way she could hide the wild response of her body to his every touch.

He unclipped her bra and dropped it to the floor, caressingly slid his hands down to her panties.

Cathy moved jerkily, arching towards him. She took his head between her hands and pulled him down towards her, her mouth searching desperately for his, a moan of satisfaction escaping from her as she found it. At the first contact Muir's lips were hard and cool, giving her nothing, then suddenly she felt him alter; his arms went round her, possessively pressing her closer, his palms flat against the supple flesh of her back, and the kiss became a heated exchange, their bodies pulsing as one being.

He picked her up and walked into the bedroom, still kissing her, laid her on the bed in the dark room, detaching his mouth with reluctance as she clung to it.

Neither of them spoke; Muir undressed with a haste that told her he was as aroused as she was, and Cathy watched him feverishly, afraid he might change his mind again, deliberately frustrate her. As he knelt on the bed she saw his face glimmering in the darkness, the eyes fixed points of light.

'I love you, Muir darling, I love you,' she groaned, lifting her arms to him, and he came down to her with a harsh intake of breath. His head burrowed between her breasts and she twisted restlessly, aching with desire. She heard him muttering something, his hand intimately sliding down her body, then he took her, and only as they moved in fierce urgency did Cathy's mind backtrack to what he had said. 'I've got to have you.'

It was the last conscious thought she had for the next few minutes. Her mind submerged as her body drove with Muir to the limit of fulfilment; tangled together, skin on skin, her hands moving from his hair to his nape, sliding down his spine, their movements convulsive at last, clutching, gripping him closer, while Muir groaned and drove into her with his cheek forced against her face, his skin burning. When the mounting spiral reached the peak Cathy's ears began to hear again, her mind picked up the sobbing escape breaking out of her, the uncontrolled cries as she burst through the barrier of self into the abandonment of falling freely through the air, and Muir's husky voice in counterpoint, groaning.

She felt intensely sad as the pleasure faded. Muir lay on her, his face hot on her breast, his body shuddering and breathing quickly. Cathy closed her arms around him and kissed his hair. 'I love you.'

She could not bear it if he looked at her coldly now, if she saw that hatred in his eyes, felt him rejecting her.

He moved away, turned on his side and leaned his head on his elbow to look down at her.

'I didn't lie, Muir,' she said pleadingly. 'I really did have amnesia, I swear I did. I was guilty about Stephen, it was such a mess, I didn't know what to do—I was split right down the middle. I couldn't face the decision, I suppose—maybe part of me knew I was deliberately forgetting, but it wasn't a conscious part, I didn't lie knowingly.'

He brushed the tangled hair back from her face, and nodded. 'I believe you.'

She stared uncertainly. 'You do?'

'I think I knew you had amnesia when I followed you to Garth House and you looked at me with that stunned expression. You have a very expressive face, I can read every thought on it. I

was too angry to think about it then, I only knew I
wanted to hurt you, but I've thought about it
since, and you looked as if you'd just dropped
through a hole in the world.'

'That was how I felt—it all came rushing back
at once and I was staggered. All the time while I
had amnesia I felt so guilty and worried. I couldn't
find out why I felt like that, I only knew
something terrible had happened and I was in
trouble. When I saw you, I remembered at once,
but I honestly didn't know about the police.
You've got to believe me—I wouldn't have done
that to you.'

Muir looked into her anxious eyes, and
grimaced. 'I know. Half of what I've said to you
since then has been sheer wind and fury. I wanted
to hurt you as much as you'd hurt me—I wasn't
thinking rationally. I was just hitting out in all
directions like a crazy man.' His mouth twisted
with rueful self-mockery. 'And I was being a bit of
an opportunist, too, if we're being frank.'

Cathy stared, frowning. 'What do you mean?'

'It was the perfect blackmail situation,' said
Muir, his mouth wry. 'I was bitterly angry with
you, but I knew I still wanted you. I was given a
chance to get you away from Telford and marry
you—and I took it.'

Her mouth rounded on a gasp. 'Were you
acting?'

He considered that, his head on one side. 'Not
exactly, no. Slightly schitzoid, maybe—at times I
wasn't quite sure whether I loved or hated you,
but however I felt, it was pretty violent.' His smile
went and his eyes were sombre. 'You don't know

how much you hurt me. When they told me you denied knowing me I felt as though someone had just kicked me in the stomach, I bled all over the floor.'

Cathy bit her lip. 'I'm so sorry, Muir,' she whispered. 'Forgive me.'

He bent over and kissed her lingeringly, his finger gentle on her throat. 'I may—in time,' he whispered. 'You'll have to be very nice to me, though.' His voice teased, invited, his hands made his meaning very plain, and Cathy felt her heart miss a beat.

'Muir, when you said you thought I'd been using you . . . that I'd meant to provoke you into making love to me and then blame you—that wasn't true! I really was torn in half over what to do, I was so fond of Stephen and I knew how much he needed me. It was a situation I couldn't cope with—I wanted you, I loved you, but I couldn't make the choice.' She was stammering, her face distressed, and Muir put a finger on her lips, nodding.

'I know. It was a damnable situation to be in—for all three of us—but, Cathy, the only way out was to cut the Gordian knot, break free by force. That was why I blackmailed you into coming away with me. I knew I had to do it then or you would have fallen back into the same trap. Pity is dangerous. Telford wouldn't have wanted your pity. He must be a tough guy or he could never have fought his way back the way he has. A man who can do what he's done is the last man who'll accept a woman's pity if he's in love with her.'

'He said he refused to hate me just because I'm

human,' she whispered. 'He said he'd been expecting it, that's why he would never get married until he could walk, he refused to marry me until he was perfectly fit again.'

'He's quite a guy,' Muir commented. 'If I wasn't still jealous of him I'd even like him.'

Cathy half laughed, half sighed. 'You don't have any cause to be jealous of him.'

'No?' Muir's hand caressed her and she quivered.

'No,' she said huskily, stroking his shoulder with answering passion.

'I'm a man who likes proof of everything,' Muir said. 'I learnt my journalism in a hard school— never accept a statement until you've checked that it's accurate, that's my motto.'

Cathy laughed, her lashes fluttering with teasing amusement. 'So?'

'So—show me,' he said.

A WORD ABOUT THE AUTHOR

Since she began writing for Harlequin Presents in late 1978, Charlotte Lamb has had close to forty books in this series published. Her explanation for this tremendous volume of superb romance writing is simple: "I love to write, and it comes very easily to me."

Once Charlotte has begun a story, the plot, the actions and the personalities of the characters unfold effortlessly and spontaneously, as her quick fingers commit the ideas of her fertile imagination to paper.

And so, in her beautiful old home on the rain-swept, uncrowded Isle of Man, where she lives with her husband and five children, Charlotte spends eight hours a day at her typewriter spinning love stories—and enjoying every minute of it!

Her career as a writer has opened many doors for her, and travel is one of them. Yet despite all the countries she has visited and enjoyed in the past few years, her greatest love is still London, the city where she was born and raised.

DISCOVER...

SUPERROMANCE

From the publisher that understands how you feel about love.

Almost 400 pages of outstanding romance reading in every book!

For a truly SUPER read, don't miss...

SUPERROMANCE

EVERYTHING YOU'VE ALWAYS WANTED A LOVE STORY TO BE!

Contemporary!
A modern romance for the modern woman—set in the world of today.

Sensual!
A warmly passionate love story that reveals the beautiful feelings between a man and a woman in love.

Dramatic!
An exciting and dramatic plot that will keep you enthralled till the last page is turned.

Exotic!
The thrill of armchair travel—anywhere from the majestic plains of Spain to the towering peaks of the Andes.

Satisfying!
Almost 400 pages of romance reading—a long satisfying journey you'll wish would never end.

SUPERROMANCE